LOVE, I THOUGHT YOU HAD MY BACK

AN URBAN ROMANCE

A Novel by
Shanice B.

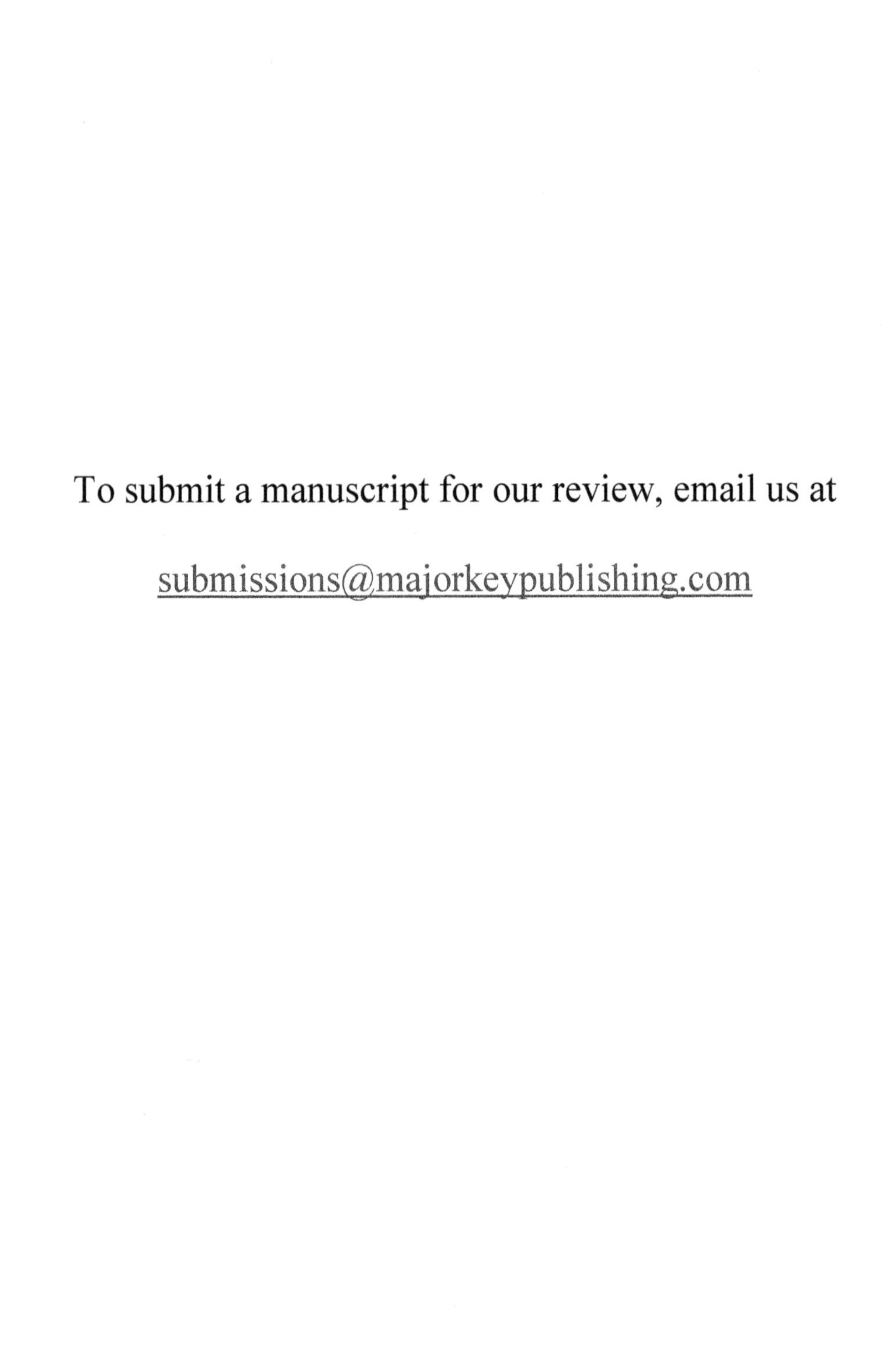

To submit a manuscript for our review, email us at

submissions@majorkeypublishing.com

Published by Major Key Publishing

www.majorkeypublishing.com

Contains explicit language & adult themes suitable for ages 16+

Be sure to LIKE our Major Key Publishing

page on Facebook!

DEDICATION

TO THE MAN WHO HAS HELD ME DOWN SINCE DAY ONE, I LOVE YOU.

BOOKS BY SHANICE B.

•LOVE ME IF YOU CAN

•LOVE ME IF YOU CAN 2

•LOVE ME IF YOU CAN 3

•WHO'S BETWEEN THE SHEETS: MARRIED TO A CHEATER

•WHO'S BETWEEN THE SHEETS: MARRIED TO A CHEATER 2

•WHO'S BETWEEN THE SHEETS: MARRIED TO A CHEATER 3

•WHO'S BETWEEN THE SHEETS: MARRIED TO A CHEATER 4

•LOVING MY MR. WRONG: A STREET LOVE AFFAIR 1

•LOVING MY MR. WRONG: A STREET LOVE AFFAIR 2

•A LOVE SO DEEP: NOBODY ELSE ABOVE YOU (STANDALONE)

•STACKING IT DEEP: MARRIED TO MY PAPER

•KISS ME WHERE IT HURTS 1

•KISS ME WHERE IT HURTS 2

•KISS ME WHERE IT HURTS 3

- HE LOVES THE SAVAGE IN ME
- HE LOVES THE SAVAGE IN ME 2

SOMETIMES YOU GOT TO FORGET WHAT YOU FEEL AND REMEMBER WHAT YOU DESERVE.

-KEYSHIA COLE

Princess

2007

I had just stepped into the house when I heard loud banging and screaming coming from my mom's room. I quickly dropped my book bag on the couch before I headed toward her bedroom to make sure she was okay. My heart began to beat erratically as I neared her bedroom door. I pushed the door open and was shocked to see my mom giving head while another man was hitting her from the back. I stood there frozen until her eyes met mine. I saw the anger in her eyes as she pushed the dick that she was sucking out her mouth and walked over to me half naked.

"Why the fuck are you standing here like you stupid? Get the fuck out of here!"

"I heard you scream. I thought you was…"

Smack.

I fell to the floor in shock as she stared down at me. I touched my left cheek as tears fell from my eyes.

"Get the fuck out of my damn room," she spat at me.

I screamed out as she grabbed me by my arm, dragged me off the floor, and slammed her door in my face.

I stood there outside her door in disbelief until I heard her screaming out yet again. I wiped the tears from my eyes as I ran out the front door and headed toward my best friend's house. It was the month of December, and it was cold outside. I was dressed in a pair of blue jeans, some black boots, and a black long-sleeved sweater. I shivered as I began to walk the block to Janae's house. All I truly ever wanted was to feel loved, but I never once got that from either of my parents. Growing up in the projects was hard enough, but having a mother who didn't give a shit about me and a father who didn't care to speak two words to me was what really hurt me to my soul. I found myself praying to God every night to make my pain go away and every day I opened my eyes to the same shit. I was only fourteen years old, and I had no one I could trust but my best friend Janae.

Janae and I had been best friends since the third grade, and when shit would get hard at home I always would go over to her house to spend a few nights until I felt it was safe enough to go back home. Today wasn't any different. I rubbed my hands together as I tried to keep them warm, but it wasn't any use. The cold breeze wasn't showing any mercy to my slim frame.

I pulled out my cell and was just about to text Janae to let her know I was on my way over to her house when I heard a car behind me banging “Pussy Money Weed” by Lil’ Wayne. I turned around and wasn’t shocked to see my daddy riding in his black and white Dodge Charger with the tinted windows. There was no other car in Warner Robins that was made like my father’s. There would have been a time that I would have waved him down in hopes he would pick me up and spend some father-daughter time with me. I never got that wish.

I was just about to turn the corner when he blew his horn at me. I turned around thinking that he was going to stop and give me a ride, but my heart sank when he sped by without even stopping.

“Bastard,” I mumbled.

I never understood why my mom never asked him for a dime. Instead, all she did was get high on drugs and alcohol and fuck any nigga that was willing to give her some coins instead of making my dad do something for me. This nigga kept money in his pockets, and word on the street was my daddy was hustling on the block. I knew they were just rumors, but it had to be true because his ass didn’t have a job, but he was still riding in style and rocking name brand clothes from his head all the way down to his toes. Not once had he ever done anything for me. Since I had been on this earth, he had only given me twenty dollars, and my mom didn't even give it to me. Instead, she took it from me to go and buy her some drugs.

I was grateful to see Janae's house in the distance. I swiftly walked the rest of the way until I was able to knock on her door. When the door opened and Janae peeked her head out, she quickly embraced me in a hug. I must have looked crazy as hell because she immediately asked what had happened to me.

"Me and mom got into it. Do you think I can chill with you for a few hours?"

"Of course, you know you can come over anytime," Janae said gently as she ushered me inside.

Stepping into Janae's place was like stepping into another world. Even though she too was staying in the projects, her mom didn't act like mine did. Her mom worked two jobs and was rarely home while my mom couldn't even hold down a minimum wage job. Janae was mostly by herself part of the day, and she didn't mind me coming over to keep her company.

I headed toward the bathroom so I could wipe my tear stained cheeks. After I washed my face and pulled my weave back into a ponytail, I headed toward the living room where Janae was sitting down watching TV.

A few moments later I followed Janae into the kitchen, and we both decided to cook us a pizza in the oven. We had just placed the pizza on the oven rack when we heard over ten shots coming from outside. Janae and I both stared at one another in fear. Whenever we heard that many shots, it only meant one thing. We quickly slammed the oven door shut before we ran toward the living room and pulled back the curtains to see what had happened.

"Ain't that your dad's car?" Janae asked curiously.

I squinted my eyes, and that's when I noticed his Dodge Charger in the middle of the street. Janae and I both looked at one another before we ran toward the front door and toward the crowd that had gathered in the streets. I could hear the ambulance and police sirens in the distance. They were on their way, and I just prayed they weren't too late. Janae and I squeezed through the crowd that had gathered outside, and that's when I noticed my dad lying in a pool of his own blood. His car was shot up, and the windows were busted out. I stood there and looked down at him as he stared back into my eyes.

He tried speaking, but blood sputtered from his mouth. I looked back at Janae who was staring at me as if she had seen a ghost. I got down on my knees as his hand gripped mine. I was just about to place my ear toward his mouth when he grew still. The ambulance pulled up a few seconds later, but it was too late. My dad was dead. I stood there and didn't shed a tear as they zipped his body up in a black body bag.

Princess

2017

I groaned in irritation when I looked down at my work schedule. I was sick and tired of working at KFC and having this crazy ass schedule. I had spoken to my manager about putting me on nights because I wanted to go back to school during the day so I could get a better job, but my manager wasn't bothered about my requests. Instead, she kept my schedule where I was working all these crazy ass hours and didn't even have time to enroll in school. I didn't want to be stuck working at a minimum wage job when I could be doing so much more with my life.

Because I had bills that needed to be paid, there was no way I was going to quit the only job I had just to go back to school at this moment. I guess I was going to have to put school off for a little while longer.

I had just clocked out and was on my way out the door when my phone began to blast "Sweet" by Travis Scott. I started to ignore it but picked up just in case it was an important call.

"Hello?"

"Princess, this your mama. How you been?"

I was silent for a moment because I hadn't talked to my mom in over a year. She was the last person I was expecting to hear from. The last time she and I had spoken, we had gotten into an argument. She had stolen over $500 from my purse and spent it on drugs and alcohol. Even though my mom had made my childhood a living hell, I still cared about her and her welfare. I had tried on different occasions to get my mom clean, and every time I sent her to rehab, she always ended up leaving and going right back to getting high.

"Baby, are you still there? I know you don't want to have anything to do with me, but honey, I really need you."

I closed my eyes for a moment as I thought back to my past.

I was only ten years old. I had just come home and found no food in the fridge and the lights disconnected. I tried turning on the water, but there was no water either.

"Mom," I called out to her, but I got no answer.

I walked toward her room and watched her from the hallway as she snorted her a few lines of white stuff up her nose. I stared at her for only a moment before I walked into my room and shut the door behind me. This wasn't the first time that I had come home and didn't have any food and the lights disconnected. A few moments later, I heard a man's voice and then her laughing. I rolled my eyes and placed the pillow over my face as I dozed off into a deep sleep. I don't know how long I slept before I woke up.

I woke up to a growling stomach and the urge to pee. I had just slid out of bed and was heading toward the bathroom when I heard my mother's door open and then close. I looked behind me, and I noticed the man who must have been talking with my mom earlier before I went to sleep. I didn't speak. Instead, I tried to hurry toward the bathroom.

After I left the bathroom, I cracked open the door and was happy to know that I was by myself. At least that was what I thought until I entered my bedroom and noticed he was sitting on my bed.

"What are you doing in here?" I choked out.

The man was dark-skinned, muscular, and was rocking a low fade. He grinned, and his gold-plated grill gleamed in the moonlight.

"Don't be acting shy. I'm not going to hurt you. I'm your mother's friend."

He grabbed me by my arm, and I quickly tried to pull away which made him aggressive. He didn't hesitate to push me down on the bed and cover my mouth so I wouldn't scream.

"You such a pretty little girl," the man slurred into my ear.

I wanted to throw up as his breath brushed up against my ear. I began to pray a silent prayer to the man above as the dude tore off my shorts and pulled down his pants. Tears fell from my eyes because I wasn't stupid. I knew what was about to happen. I tried fighting him, but there was no use. He was just way too strong.

He smacked me in the face which brought more tears to my eyes.

"Be still. It won't hurt," he mumbled in my ear as he began to stroke his dick with his free hand. He was just about to stick it in when his phone began to ring. He pulled his phone out of his pocket and looked down at the screen as he looked back at me.

I was relieved when he quickly slid off of me and answered on the second ring. I had no clue who it was that called him, but I was grateful that he had gotten off of me. A few moments later, he ended the call and looked back at me.

"I have to run, but we will be seeing each other again."

I shivered as he walked out my room. I found it hard to go back to sleep. Instead, I laid in bed and cried until sleep found me. The next day, when I tried telling my mom about what happened, she told me that I was a liar and slapped me in the face. My feelings were hurt because never would I ever lie to her about something that serious. I knew right then that my mother didn't give two fucks about me. I was lucky enough that my mother never brought him back over to her house. It wasn't because of me, but because she found her drugs cheaper somewhere else.

I wanted a healthy relationship with my mom. However, I had finally accepted that the relationship that my mom and I had was toxic, and it wasn't going to change anytime soon.

"Are you still there, Princess?"

The line went quiet, and I pulled the phone from my ear to see if she was still on the phone.

"Mom, are you there?"

"Yes, I'm here."

I could tell by her voice that something was wrong with her. I became tense when I heard her crying into the phone.

"Baby, I really need to talk with you face to face. Can you meet me somewhere?"

By now, my mind was running a mile a minute because I didn't know what was going on. I had never heard my mom cry.

My head told me to tell her to fuck off because she didn't deserve my love or my concern, but my heart told me to find out what was going on with her because even though she had been a sorry ass mom when I was growing up, she still was my family.

"Yes, we can meet," I heard myself say.

"Meet me in front of Golden Corral at 9:00 p.m.," my mom spoke into the phone.

After she had ended the call, I still couldn't get over the fact that my mom had finally reached out to me, but I also had the feeling that something was wrong with her.

I hurried out of KFC so I could hurry home and hop in the tub before I met my mom later that night.

*****

I had been on my feet for eight hours, and I was aching all over, so I decided to soak in the tub before I headed to Golden Corral. Tank filled my bathroom as I closed my eyes and let the rose scented bubble bath caress my caramel skin. After over thirty minutes of soaking, I stepped out the tub and wrapped my body in a big purple towel. I tiptoed into my bedroom so I could pick something out to wear. After ten minutes of looking through my closet, I finally decided to put on a pair of skinny jeans, my brown ankle boots, and a brown sweater. I brushed my teeth, flat ironed my Remy weave, and put a little makeup on my face. I took a few pictures of myself before I posted them on my Instagram.

It wasn't even five minutes before my phone began dinging and niggas started posting comments about how sexy I looked. I chuckled as I slid my phone into my pocket. I wasn't going to lie; a bitch was looking fine as hell. I was thick in all the right places, medium height, and had a big juicy booty that a nigga could grab on. I had hips, sexy thighs, and I had enough titties that a nigga could use them as a pillow if he wanted to. I dabbed a little lip gloss on my lips before I took one last picture of myself and headed out my front door.

The closer I got to Golden Corral the more I began to worry about what my mom had to tell me. By the time I pulled my black Acura into the turning lane, I noticed just how packed it was. Damn, it was a Thursday night, but it looked like it was a Saturday night. I pulled out my phone and punched in the number that my mom had called me from earlier. She picked up on the first ring.

"Princess, have you made it here yet?"

"Yes, I'm outside. It's packed as hell out here. It's hard for me to find a parking spot."

"Well, I'm inside. I was hungry, so I decided that it would be nice that you and I could talk through dinner."

I had been working all day and had gone straight home to relax and take a bath. I had just realized that I was hungry, and it was time for me to eat.

"Sounds good."

After I had finally found somewhere to park, I hopped out and headed inside to find my mom waiting for me on the far back. My mom was medium in height, with wide hips, a flat stomach, and a caramel complexion like myself. When her hazel eyes met mine, I was taken back by how good she looked. The last time that I saw my mother, her hair was falling out, her skin was peeling, and she looked very frail. When she stood up and embraced me in a hug her sweet-scented perfume tickled my nose. She was dressed in a green sweater dress with a pair of black ankle boots and had her long weave pulled up in a bun on top of her head.

She pulled away from me as she and I both headed toward the buffet where we filled our plates with our favorite foods. After our plates were filled, we headed back to our table and took a seat. The waiter took our drink order, and we hurried to dig into our food. I was grateful that my mom didn't mention anything serious because I wanted to at least enjoy my food before we had to talk. After we were full, she leaned back in her chair as she sipped her iced tea.

"The reason I called you today is that I first want to tell you how sorry I am for everything that I did to you when you were growing up. I know that you and I haven't had the best relationship, but I want you to know that I'm a changed woman, and I want us to get to know one another."

I stared at her in disbelief because I would have never thought I was going to hear my mother say anything like this.

"I know I wasn't the best mom, and I never was there when you needed me. I just want you to know that you will never have to worry about me walking out your life. I have done a lot of shit that I'm not proud of. All I'm asking for is your forgiveness and a chance to prove to you that I've changed."

I nodded my head as I played with my uneaten mashed potatoes.

"I never thought that I would ever hear you say how sorry you were for making my life a living hell," I choked out.

"Baby, I'm sorry for that. I know it's a long time coming, but it wasn't right how I did you. I know that now. I was lost, and I was hurt. I had no love to give you because I didn't love myself. Please forgive me."

"Mom, I never once had any hate in my heart for you. All I ever wanted for you to do was be a mom to me since I didn't have a dad to pick up where you slacked off. I grew up alone with no guidance. I'm going through life not knowing shit about how to love someone. I never once experienced that emotion."

My mother looked away as she wiped a tear from her eye.

"I'm sorry, honey. I'm really am. I can't go back and turn back the hands of time and give you the nurturing that I didn't give you when you were growing up."

"Yeah, I know you can't, and I've accepted that. I just need to know two things, and please, be honest with me."

"What do you want to know?" my mom asked seriously.

"Are you still doing drugs?"

My mom looked away from me, and my heart began to ache. I already knew her answer even before she said a word.

"Yes, I'm still using, but it isn't an everyday thing. I'm doing so much better. Back in the day, I had to get high all day every day. Now, I'm only getting high every other day or when I feel stressed."

I glared at her for only a moment, and I could see that she was definitely telling the truth. She looked better. She seemed to be taking good care of herself, and at the end of the day, that was all I really carried about. Doing drugs was an addiction, and it wasn't something a person could just stop at a drop of a dime. It was a process, and I understood the struggle that she was going through. All that mattered to me was that she was trying to make a change.

"Mom, I'm proud that you are cutting back on the drugs."

"Baby, I honestly appreciate everything you have done to try to get me clean. All the money you spent on me really showed me that someone out there cared about my well-being. I just was in a bad place, and I wasn't ready yet."

I nodded my head as I played with my napkin because the next question I wanted to ask her was really the one I had been waiting years to ask her. I just didn't know exactly how to spit it out because I was scared of what she was going to say to me.

When she reached across the table and grabbed my hand, I looked up at her and could see the worry and pain in her eyes.

"What's the matter, honey? Is something bothering you?"

"I need to know why my dad never was there for me."

My mother pulled away from me and looked away for a moment. She stared over at the black couple who was feeding some mashed potatoes to one of their children.

"I met your father when I was only twenty years old. He was the finest man on the block, and at the time, all the girls wanted him. I fell in love with him instantly. I knew time I laid eyes on him that he was going to be the man I was going to spend the rest of my life with. My parents hated him because he didn't have a job and had no education. They had always been the type of people who believed that the man was always supposed to be the provider of the family. Because he lacked the qualities of being successful in life by getting a nine to five job, they didn't allow me to date him. But me being young and thinking that I was in love, I still dated him and gave him my heart. Your father was a real street nigga and was making major moves. He had so much money that you could swim in it. It wasn't legal money; it was dirty money. At the time, I didn't care.

I was only twenty-one years old when I first rolled and smoked my first blunt. I was twenty-two when I popped my first pill, and I was twenty-three when I first tried cocaine. Your father was there with me every time I got high and made sure that I never overdosed on any of his product. I was the one who took the sample just to see how good the product was. I got addicted, and that's when shit got ugly. I dropped out of college when I found out I was pregnant with you. That's also when I found out that he was cheating on me with all different types of bitches.

After I gave birth to you, I began getting high on the regular, and he was barely coming home at night. I cried myself to sleep every night and woke the next morning to repeat it all over again. I wasn't happy. I was struggling to make a man love me who never loved me from the beginning. Your father eventually left me for one of our neighbors, and I lost all sense of reality after that. Every day that I laid in bed, I told myself that I should have listened to my parents when they told me to leave him alone. I had no job, no skills, no education, and I was a single mother. There was no way I was going to be able to go back home to my parents with you, so I decided the best thing for me to do was raise you and try to make it the best way I knew how. He never once helped me with you, and after a while, I stopped asking him. I wasn't about to force anyone to do something that they didn't want to do."

I wiped the tears that had fallen from my eyes as she stood up and embraced me.

"I love you, Princess."

"I love you too, Mom," I replied emotionally.

When we pulled away from each other, I reached into my purse so I could leave a tip.

"I'm so glad that you decided to meet me tonight."

"I'm glad I did also," I said truthfully.

As I drove home, my heart felt lighter, and I was at peace. Today had turned out to be a good day after all.

CAMERON

It was 9:00 p.m. I had just jumped off the porch and was heading to the block to get my grind on. I kissed my girl goodbye and told her to hit my phone up if she needed me. I had been fucking around with Brianna for over six months, and she was holding a nigga down like we had been fucking around for years. From day one, when she learned that I was a street nigga, she never once questioned anything that I did. She was loyal as hell and for that, I promised that I was going to look out for her as well. Whatever she wanted, she didn't have to worry her pretty little head about nothing because I had her.

Time I stepped outside, I spotted Icey J waiting on me. Icey J and I had been homies since we were kids. We both grew up on the Northside of Warner Robins and went to middle school with one another. We both dropped out of high school at the age of sixteen to sell rocks on the streets. I started early selling dope, and Icey J followed my lead. I was making hella money back in high school, so I was like fuck school, and Icey J agreed. When my mom found out that I wasn't going to school, she quickly tried to intervene, but it wasn't shit that she could do. I had made up my mind, and there was nothing that she could say to change it.

I was tired of coming home to see my mom struggling to pay her bills, working twelve-hour shifts and still didn't have enough food in the fridge to keep us fed. I wanted to help out, and the only way I saw how was to sell dope on the streets. Even though my mom didn't agree, she finally got used to me going out at night, hanging out on the block, and having all types of people knocking on my window late at night.

"Nigga, you ready to get this paper?" I asked Icey J.

"Hell yeah, nigga. You know I'm down."

Icey J stood in front of his car dressed in a pair of black skinny leg jeans, black boots, a black and gray long sleeve shirt with Biggie on the front, and a black jacket to match. His dreads were pulled back in a ponytail. When he smiled, his silver-plated grill smiled back. Icey J was medium in height, slim, brown-skinned, and tatted from his neck all the way to his stomach. He constantly had bitches blowing up his phone and had them willing to cheat on their nigga to give him a sample of their pussy. Little did these hoes know, Icey J had already given his heart to someone, but these bitches didn't care about that shit. They were still trying to be the side bitch.

I dapped Icey J up before I zipped up my black and red jacket, hopped in the car with him, and headed to our trap house. We had just pulled up when we noticed the yard was deep as hell. 2 Chainz was blasting from the speakers, bitches were shaking their asses, and niggas were posted up chilling. I stepped out the car, and marijuana smoke filled my lungs. I was just about to head into the trap house with Icey J when I heard my name being called.

"Cameron, Cameron."

I turned around and saw Drea walking over to where I was posted up.

"Baby, can I get a gram of coke."

"How much money you got?"

"Um, you think you can front it to me until I get paid tomorrow?"

I looked at Drea as if she had lost her mind. I had fronted her once, and I promised I was never going to do that shit again. I wanted to murder the bitch last time because she didn't want to pay up when she got her check. I wasn't in the mood to fuck a bitch up about my paper.

"Drea, how about you come tomorrow when you get paid, and I will sell you any drug you want."

"Please, Cameron. I really need me some coke."

"Shorty, I can't help you."

"How about I do something for you?" Drea asked flirtatiously.

"Drea, there is nothing that you can do for me but get out my damn face."

Drea walked over to where I was standing and began to rub her hands over my chest. She licked her glossy lips before she whispered into my ear.

"I will suck your dick free of charge for that gram of coke."

I quickly pulled away from her. Drea wasn't an ugly bitch, but there was no way I was about to let her off the hook just because she wanted to get my dick wet. Drea was short, slender, and dark in complexion with a baby face. She was cute and all, but I wasn't the type of nigga to mix business with pleasure. After she realized that I wasn't going to give her anything free, she disappeared. Icey J shook his head as he watched her walk off.

"You didn't have what shorty wanted?"

"I had exactly what she wanted, but she ain't have any money. Ain't shit free in this world."

Icey J groaned when he pulled out his cell from his pocket. I looked over at him when I noticed his facial expression.

"Nigga, you good?"

"Yeah, I'm good. It's just this bitch I been fucking with keep blowing up my phone. She been stressing a nigga out lately."

I shook my head because Icey J always seemed to find himself in some bullshit when he started fucking around on his girl with bitches who didn't have shit to lose.

"Nigga, what have you done now?" I joked.

Icey J smiled which brought his silver-plated grill into view.

"I ain't do shit but smash this bitch. Now she wants me to be her man."

I shook my head as I laughed at him.

"Man, you done fucked up now. I told you. You can't just be fucking around with anybody. You got to fuck around only with the hoes that know their role. You always get the bitches that want to take your girl spot."

"I don't know why I always keep getting these crazy ass bitches. Every time I give them the dick, they act possessive and crazy as fuck."

"That should tell you something. You need to stop fucking around and just be loyal to your girl."

"I am loyal to my girl, but I can't help wanting a little something on the side, and nigga, don't stand here like you ain't never fucked around on Brianna."

I paused for only a moment.

"I'm not going to lie and say that I never smashed another bitch since I been fucking around with Brianna, but the one time I did fuck around, I made sure the hoe didn't know too much about me to come after my girl. To this day, Brianna don't know shit about me smashing anybody because I pick bitches that know their role. I haven't cheated on Brianna since that one time because she the only thing I want. She holds a nigga down. A nigga like us can't call everyone wifey because they ain't loyal to wear that title. You don't want to fuck around, lose your girl, and end up with a hoe who will turn on you with a drop of a dime."

"I get what you saying," Icey J mumbled.

"Yeah, so call that hoe back, and let her know she need to chill the fuck out, or you going to have to stop fucking around with her. Your loyalty is to your girl always."

Icey J nodded his head as he pulled his cell out to handle his business.

I stayed at the trap house for about an hour joking around and selling some dope before I told Icey J I was about to head to KFC to get me something to eat before they closed.

He gave me the keys to his custom made 2018 black Camaro with the chrome black rims and I gladly headed toward my destination. When I stopped at the red light I pulled out a blunt that I had rolled and lit that bitch up. "Poor Fool" by 2 Chainz blasted from the speakers as marijuana smoke filled the car. I pulled up at KFC a few moments later and made sure to put out my blunt before I hopped out the car. KFC was packed, and all eyes were on me as soon as I stepped inside. Bitches were practically drooling as I stepped in the line and waited for my turn to order. I chuckled when I heard the girl in front of me tell her friend just how fine I was.

I was dressed in a pair of red skinny leg jeans, black boots, a black and red long-sleeved shirt, and a black and red jacket. I was tall and light-skinned with long dreads that hung down my back, and I had pretty, straight white teeth. I also had light brown eyes, rocked diamonds in both my ears, and a silver stud in my nose. My looks alone attracted all types of women, but after Brianna came into my life, I decided that fucking around with all these hoes wasn't even worth it. All they cared about was my money and what I could do for them. If it wasn't benefiting them, they didn't give a damn about it.

When it was my turn to order, I stared up at the menu for a moment so I could decide what I wanted to eat. The girl in front of me was staring a nigga down like she was down to fuck a nigga right then and there. I quickly looked away from her and back at the menu because there was no way I was about to even give this bitch a chance. After I had gave the girl my order, she quickly gave me my number and told me that my order was going to be out next. I grabbed my receipt from her, and our eyes locked. She was thick, light-skinned, and had her hair pulled up in a ponytail. She was rocking her KFC cap with her name tag stuck on her shirt that said *Dee (Shift Leader)*. She smiled at me, and I immediately saw her glistening white teeth. When her hands rubbed mine I quickly pulled away, and she instantly caught the hint that I wasn't interested. She rolled her eyes at me before she dismissed me and shouted my order out to the back where the people were cooking my food. I didn't give a fuck about her being all mad. Instead, I filled my drink up with ice and poured myself some coke as I waited on my order. I was just about to text Brianna when I heard my number being called. I slid my phone back in my pocket and was on my way to the counter when I heard the Dee yelling.

"Princess, get your ass outside and clean the windows!" Dee yelled toward the back. I grabbed my food and was just about to head out the door when the girl I assumed was Princess started to get loud with Dee

"Look, Dee, I'm sick and tired of you talking to me like I'm some fucking child. You need to start putting some respect on my name. I can't be in two places at once. Just a minute ago, you told me to prep and fry chicken. Now you telling me to go outside in the damn cold to clean windows. I have been nothing but a good worker. Everyone else is barely pulling their weight around here, but you always trying to single me out. I'm tired of this shit."

"I can speak to you any way I want to. I'm the one in charge, not you. You going to do what I say, or you can get off the fucking clock," Dee spat.

I could see that the girl looked like she wanted to punch Dee, but instead, she did as she was told. To be honest, I felt sorry for the girl because she looked like she was tired as hell. She had flour smeared all over her clothes like she had been prepping chicken all day, the majority of her hair had escaped her bun, and she was sweating like crazy. I looked at her as she grabbed her jacket, the bottle of spray and a rag, and headed out the door into the cold wind. I was the only one left in the restaurant who had heard everything that had went down. Everyone else that was in line before me had already grabbed their food and left. I quickly followed Princess and was just about to step in the car when I heard her crying.

Hearing a female cry was one of my weaknesses. Growing up, I hated hearing my mom cry, and I always did whatever I could to keep a smile on her face. A part of me wanted me to dip the fuck out and head back to the trap house, but the other part of me wanted to find out why she was crying. I groaned when I placed my food on the passenger side and walked over to where Princess was sitting on the windowsill crying her eyes out.

I bent down on one knee so we would be eye level with one another.

"Lil' mama, are you okay?"

She looked up at me and quickly wiped her eyes.

"Yes, I'm good," she choked out before she stood up and tried to get back to work.

When her eyes connected with mine, I felt as if she had touched my heart with her beauty. It was something about her that had a nigga drawn to her. She was very beautiful to me. To be honest, she was perfect in my eyes. She was medium height with a creamy caramel complexion, full lips, and soft brown eyes that you could get lost in.

"What's your name, lil' mama?"

"My name is Princess." She sniffled.

"My name is Cameron."

Princess shivered as a cold breeze hit us in the face.

"I'm not trying to get in your business and all, but I saw how your shift leader was talking to you. You really need to report her to your manager."

Princess stopped what she was doing and looked up at me.

"Thanks for your concern, but Dee don't put no fear in my heart. The manager isn't going to say nothing to her about how she talk to anyone in that restaurant. I'm a big girl. I can deal with her bullshit. I've been through a lot of shit in my life. Dealing with Dee is nothing."

I raised up my hand to let her know that I was only trying to help.

"I'm sorry if it seemed like I had an attitude. It has been a long day."

"Yeah, you look like you been slaving all day. I'm sure your man is going to take good care of you when you get home."

Princess laughed.

"First off, I don't have a man, and I'm not looking for one. They come with too many damn problems. I'd rather stay by myself."

I chuckled.

"Well, since you don't have a man. Would you like for me to take you out sometimes? And before you start to have some crazy thoughts, let me add that this is not a date. I honestly want to take you out and show you a good time. That's all."

Princess looked at me with a blank expression on her face.

I was shocked as hell that I had even approached Princess, but there was something about her that I gravitated to. I didn't know exactly what it was, but I wanted to at least find out. Fucking her was the last thing on my mind. One look at her, and I knew she wasn't about that life. *I'm fascinated by her. That's all,* I told myself.

"Are you being serious?" Princess asked.

"Um, I'm serious as a heart attack"

Princes smirked.

"Well, if you paying for it, then I would be crazy to turn your offer down."

"Can I at least get your number, lil' mama, so I can hit you up sometimes?"

"Not if you keep calling me lil' mama."

She and I both laughed.

"I promise to never call you lil' mama… only Princess."

Princess rattled off her number and I saved it in my phone.

I had just saved her number when my phone began to blast Gucci Mane. I looked down and noticed it was Icey J calling me.

"What up, Icey J?"

"Nigga, where you at?"

"I got caught up, but I'm on the way back."

"Okay cool, because Drea just pulled up with her brothers. I'm about to pop these niggas if they think they about to come up in here disrespecting me."

"What the fuck? Give me five minutes. I will be there. Don't do nothing until I get there."

I disconnected the call and slid my phone back in my pocket.

I stared down at Princess, who was finally finished cleaning the windows. “It was nice meeting you, Princess. I hope you have a nice night.”

Princess gave me a weak smile.

“Thank you. I will once I clock out of here.”

“I’ma hit you up later.”

“Of course you will.” Princess chuckled as she waved goodbye.

I hopped in the car and looked back to make sure Princess had made it back inside of KFC safely before I pulled out into traffic.

Janae

A bitch was tired as hell. I had been slaving all fucking night at Cracker Barrel, and all I wanted to do was sleep the day away. I rolled over, picked up my phone, and noticed that it was 1:00 p.m. There was no way I was about to get my ass up. Instead, I pulled the covers over my head until I heard my phone began to play "Sexy" by Tank. Even though I was tired, there was no way I was about to miss a call from my man Darnell. Darnell and I had been fucking around for over two years, and I was deeply in love with him. There was no other man on this green earth that made me feel the way Darnell did. I was crazy about my man, and I always told myself that I would never let anyone come between our happiness.

My smile instantly faded from my face when I heard a female voice in my ear.

"Darnell?" I asked.

"No, bitch, this isn't Darnell. My name is Lexi, and I'm his girlfriend. I was going through his phone when I ran across your number and decided to call your ass up to see who the fuck you were. See, Darnell and I have been fucking around for over six months. So whoever you is, you need to lose my man's number because he is taken."

My eyes began to burn as tears tried to escape my eyes. Anger consumed my body, and I was ready to fuck a bitch up. I might have been asleep a few moments ago, but I was wide awake now. I never expected to get a phone call from another bitch who was fucking my damn man. Darnell had never cheated on me. At least I thought he hadn't, but apparently, I didn't know my man as well as I thought.

This bitch was bold as fuck to even call me with this bullshit, but since she wanted to get nasty, I was ready to get nasty too.

"First off, bitch, Darnell doesn't belong to you. I've been with Darnell for over two years, you stupid hoe. Therefore, I need to be the one calling your fucking ass and telling you to leave my man alone. The first thing I want to know is what the hell you doing with my man's phone?"

"What you need to be asking yourself is where your nigga at? Oops, my bad. You don't know where he at. Well, let me ease your mind. He with me, bitch. See, your man been eating and sucking my pussy all night long. I bet you didn't know that, did you?" Lexi said with attitude.

This hoe had lost her mind if she thought for one moment I was going to let her dumb ass call me and talk shit about my damn man.

"Hoe, since you so brave, get ready for me to pull up and beat your ass," I spat into phone.

I was ready to rip Darnell's dick and balls off and rip that hoe's tongue out her mouth.

I kept asking this bitch for her address, but she wouldn't give it to me. Eventually, I heard Darnell's bitch ass in the background asking her who she was on the phone with, and then the call was disconnected.

Hot tears were running down my face, but I embraced them because if I didn't, I was going to end up fucking a nigga or a bitch up. I had been so pressed on cursing Darnell's lil' bitch's ass out that I hadn't noticed Princess standing in my doorway looking confused.

"Who in the hell was you on the phone with?" Princess asked with interest.

I closed my eyes before I counted to ten and looked up at Princess who was still standing in the same position trying to figure out what was going on with me.

"I was sleep, minding my own fucking business when I gets a phone call from Darnell. Even though I was tired, I picked up so I could talk to him. Turns out, it wasn't Darnell, but it was another bitch calling my damn phone telling me that she has been fucking my man for six months. Apparently, he with that hoe at this very moment."

There was nothing else that I could say before Princess walked over to where I was sitting and embraced me. I was more angry than sad, but I couldn't stop the tears from falling from my eyes.

"Don't worry about that nigga, Janae. You got too much shit going for yourself to be crying over a fuck boy."

"I love him, though." I cried on Princess's shoulders.

Princess rubbed her hands through my weave as she comforted me.

"Love don't suppose to hurt, boo," Princess spoke softly into my ear. I pulled away from Princess as she wiped my eyes. "I know you love him. I think the best thing for you to do is wait until he brings his ass home and find out what is really going on. Right, now you just got half the story from the bitch who probably snuck and grabbed his phone while he was taking a shower."

My heart felt as if it had been stabbed multiple times. This had to be a dream. No, this couldn't be true. I was going to wake up and find Darnell next to me, holding me as he rubbed on my booty.

"Instead of sitting here crying and being depressed, we going out," Princess ordered.

"I don't feel like going anywhere," I grumbled.

"Bitch, if you don't get your ass up and hop in the shower. We ain't about to sit here and keep talking about Darnell. I'm taking you out. I just got paid. I'm willing to blow my whole check if you down to come along with me."

I swear, Princess knew all the right things to do and say to make a bitch feel better.

"I guess I don't have no choice but to get up then."

"Yep, so go put on something sexy, and let's spend some money."

I slid out of bed as I hopped in the shower and let the hot water caress my tired and achy body. As I closed my eyes, I couldn't help but think of Darnell and how we first met.

It was the summer of 2015, and I was working at Ruby Tuesday as a waitress. It was a Saturday night, and it was one of the busiest nights of the week. Darnell was there with a few of his friends, and they seemed to be in a deep conversation when I walked over and introduced myself as their waitress for that evening. I took their drink and food orders before I headed back to the back to give the orders to the cooks.

As soon as Darnell's eyes met mine, I felt the chemistry. Darnell was sexy as hell, and I was barely able to do my job because he was a distraction. He was tall, muscular, the complexion of dark chocolate, and rocked dreads that hung down his back with a silver stud nose ring. When he smiled, I noticed his gold and silver-plated grill.

Darnell stared at me the whole time I worked the table. Every time I circled by to make sure he and his friends were enjoying their food, he always asked me something about myself. The first time I came by, he asked my age. The second time, he asked what I liked to do when I wasn't working. The third time, he asked if I had a man, and when I came by for the last time to hand him the check, he quickly grabbed me by my wrist and asked if he could have my number. A bitch was in shock and couldn't even find the words to even answer him. He stared into my eyes, and he was all I saw. I mumbled off my number and watched as he entered it into his phone.

My heart fluttered as he stood up and told me that he was going to text me later that night. I could remember that I could barely get through the rest of my shift without thinking about him. When it was time for me to clock out, my phone dinged in my pocket, and my heart skipped a beat when I saw that it was from him. Darnell and I talked all the way until the next morning.

Fast forward to two years later, and I never pictured myself with anyone but Darnell. Now that I was aware that he was entertaining another bitch, I didn't know what to do. My heart was aching, and I felt as if I was going to be sick. My heart felt broken, and I couldn't do anything but cry. After I was all cried out, I stepped out the shower and began to dry my body off before I headed back toward my bedroom to get dressed for the day.

It wasn't long before I decided what I was going to wear. I picked out a red and black sweater dress that hugged my curves and paired it with a pair of black boots that went up my leg. I put on my silver charmed necklace and earrings. I flat ironed my Brazilian weave until it was bone straight and made sure to put a little makeup on my milk chocolate skin. I didn't want anyone to see that I had been crying for over an hour straight. I applied a little eyeliner, mascara, and some red matte lipstick before I was satisfied with my appearance. I snapped a few pictures just before Princess stepped into my room and asked if I was ready to head out.

"Damn, bitch, you looking good as hell. You stepping out looking like you searching for a man."

I chuckled as I rolled my eyes.

"You looking fly also," I complimented Princess.

Princess was rocking a pair of black and white leggings, a black sweater, and a pair of tall black boots. She was stunning. She had on some silver jewelry, and her weave was pulled away from her face in a low ponytail. Her lipstick was popping, and she was looking like she was ready to pull her a few niggas too. I was just about to grab my wallet, but Princess told me to leave it at home.

"You don't need no money. I told you, I got you."

"Princess, you ain't got to do all this."

"You like a sister to me, so you already know I'm going to look out for you," Princess replied truthfully.

I nodded my head as I followed her out to her car.

"Where are you taking me?"

"First, we going to the mall to do some shopping. I made $500 slaving at KFC, so you already know I'm going to shop until I can't swipe my plastic no more."

I looked over at Princess and laughed. She always knew how to keep a smile on my face. Ten minutes later, we pulled up at the mall and looked around for a good twenty minutes before Princess's iPhone began to ring.

When Princess gasped, I looked up at her to see what was up with her. I watched as she smiled and began texting someone.

"Who got you smiling like that?" I asked her nosily.

Princess looked up, and that's when I noticed the twinkle of happiness in her eyes.

"It's someone I met at my job last night."

I placed my hands on my hips as I stared at her in disbelief.

"Bitch, I know damn well you ain't going to stand here and hold all that tea in. I want to know why in the hell you ain't been tell me about you meeting someone on your job."

Princess rolled her eyes.

"I didn't tell you because I didn't know for sure if he was even going to text me."

"Who in the hell is he?"

I was in the process of looking at some shirts but quickly turned my attention to my best friend.

I wanted to hear this damn tea. Princess had sworn up and down that she was done with men. For six months straight, Princess hadn't talked about a man or indicated that she wanted one. After Hakeem left her for one of his side pieces, Princess hadn't been the same since. I understood the pain that Princess was going through because I was going through it myself. Princess had been in love with Hakeem. She gave that nigga her all, but he still wasn't satisfied with her. Princess and Hakeem had dated for a year, and the whole time they dated, I couldn't name one time Hakeem wasn't trying to stick his dick into any bitch that was down to fuck.

Princess was a wonderful person and an amazing friend. I hated to see her depressed and barely able to function. I was so glad when she finally kicked Hakeem to the left and decided that being single was the best option for herself and her sanity.

Even though I was upset about my relationship, that didn't stop me from wanting to know about Princess and her new-found happiness. I had never been a hating ass bitch. If Princess was happy, then I was happy for her ass.

"Before you start telling me the story, make sure you don't leave shit out. I want to know every damn thing," I joked.

"You know you my bitch. You know I got you." Princess laughed.

Princess slid her phone back in her pocket before she began to tell me about the new nigga she had just recently met.

"I was slaving my ass away in the back when Dee's bitch ass yelled at me from the front to go outside to wash the windows in the fucking cold. I hate that bitch. She had been giving me a hard time the whole fucking day, but I did my best to keep my cool. The bitch had me running around KFC like I was crazy all yesterday. She didn't know what the fuck she wanted me to do. First, she wanted me to drop chicken. Then, she wanted a bitch to prep. Lastly, she wanted a bitch to go outside in the freezing cold to wash the windows down. Anyway, when she told me to wash the windows, she said it to me with an attitude. Me being me, I snapped on her ass and basically told her that I was tired of her talking to me like I was a kid—"

I held my hand up, cutting Princess off mid-sentence.

"Princess, I'm so sick of that bitch, Dee, you seriously need to be thinking about getting you another job for real. That bitch have no respect for nobody."

"I know she don't, Janae. The bitch is straight evil. I swear I wanted to lay that bitch out on the floor, but I need my job, so I took my ass outside to do what she told me to. Anyway, I was tired and frustrated, so I sat down on the windowsill so I could clear my head. That's when he came up to me and asked me if I was okay."

"Who is he?" I asked with excitement.

"He told me his name was Cameron. I mean, I couldn't even ask him his last name because I couldn't get over how sexy he was. I mean this nigga is fine as hell."

I rolled my eyes because Princess's fine and my fine was two different things. When she was dating Hakeem, I didn't know what she saw in him. I mean, the nigga wasn't ugly, but I thought that nigga had a little sugar in his tank. When Princess would be crying about his ass cheating, the first thought in the back of my mind was that he was probably cheating on her with not only women but also men. It was just something about him that gave me a vibe that he wasn't all the way straight, but I had no proof.

Princess and I liked two different type of niggas, but I guess that was a good thing that we did because we never had trouble with one of us liking the other's man. See, I liked my niggas to be hood and street while Princess liked her men to have education and not have a criminal record. She wasn't about to get herself tied up with no street nigga period.

I must have been looking at Princess crazily because she quickly asked if I was okay.

"Yes, I'm good. I'm just curious to know how he looks because your fine and my fine are totally different."

Princess's eyes sparkled.

"Cameron is sexy. A blind bitch can tell you that. He's tall, slim, light-skinned with a silver stud in his nose and diamonds in both his ears. He have light brown eyes, with straight white teeth, and he rocking some long ass dreads that hang down his back."

I clapped my hands, and Princess laughed at my ass.

"Why in the hell are you clapping your hands?" Princess asked.

"Because I think that you have finally scooped you up a nigga who might look decent."

Princess smirked.

"Well, I'm going to see where it goes. I'm not going to rush anything. You know after what happened with Hakeem, I want to take things slow."

"Ain't nothing wrong with that, boo. Take your time and have some fun. Consider Hakeem a lesson learned."

Princess and I shopped until we couldn't carry another bag. We headed over to the food court and ate some Chinese food as we talked and laughed with one another about growing up in the projects. After we were full, we grabbed our bags and headed back to the car.

We was just about to step in the car when my heart dropped. Tank began to blast from my phone, and I knew exactly who was calling me. I didn't want to answer but my heart wouldn't allow it. I dug my hand in my purse and pulled out my iPhone so I could answer Darnell's call.

I placed the phone to my ear, and my heart broke when I heard Darnell's voice.

"Baby, are you there? Look, I know I have a lot of shit to explain. I'm so sorry for everything."

Tears fell down my cheeks because I could barely even get one word out of my mouth. I was just too hurt. Instead of holding the phone to my ear, I quickly disconnected the call and hopped in the car with Princess.

Princess stared at me with sadness in her eyes, but she didn't speak. Instead, she focused her eyes on the road as we headed home

Darnell continued to blow up my phone, but I was being petty as hell and ignoring all of his calls. I mean, I didn't want to say anything to him until I had my emotions in check. I was still trying to get my mind to wrap around the fact that he was actually cheating on me with another bitch. As soon as Princess pulled up at our apartment, I saw Darnell's 2018 pearl white Cadillac with chrome rims.

"What you want to do, Janae? You want me to tell him to leave?"

"Nawl, Princess. I might as well handle this shit and get it over with."

Princess nodded her head as she and I both stepped out of her Acura.

Darnell stepped out his car and walked over to where I was standing. He spoke to Princess, but she only stared at him like he was crazy. She turned back toward me and told me if I needed her, she was going to be in the house. I waited until Princess closed the door before my eyes met Darnell's.

DARNELL

A nigga had truly fucked up, and I didn't know how to get my ass out of the situation that I found myself in. I loved Janae with all my heart, but I couldn't resist fucking around with other bitches. I knew I was wrong, and I had tried so hard to tame my urge, but I had slipped up and got caught up. When Janae and I met, I fell in love immediately. I couldn't resist just how beautiful she was inside and out. She had stuck by me and held me down from day one. When Janae and I had first met two years ago, I barely had a hundred dollars to my name, and I was living paycheck to paycheck. I was working at Krystal's doing what I could to make ends meet and slanging dope on the corner at night.

I was grateful to Janae because I no longer had to work a nine to five and still struggle to pay my bills. Janae helped me get on my feet last year by taking out a small loan to get my car washing business up and running. I made sure to pay her back every cent that she had given me. I was now the owner of Bustin' Bubble's Car Washing Services which was located on Watson Boulevard. This wasn't your average car wash either. My car wash was different, and it stood out from all the other car washes that had saturated Warner Robins. My business consisted of young women and men from the ages of eighteen to thirty who were willing to wash cars inside a secured building.

Before I hired anyone, I made sure they signed documents stating whatever happened at Bustin' Bubbles Car Wash didn't leave the facility. I hired two different types of employees. One set of employees was okay with showing parts of their bodies while they washed a customer's car for a set fee while the other set of employees didn't.

If the customer didn't have the money to be entertained, they still got their car washed, but they just would only see my employees who preferred to be fully clothed while working. Now that I was making shit loads of money, my relationship with Janae was now crumbling before my eyes.

I hated that I had ever started fucking with Lexi in the first place. When Lexi and I first met, she had come to my car wash looking sexy as hell. I could barely take my eyes off of her. She was just that mesmerizing. Lexi was dark chocolate, tall, thick in all the right places, and could suck a dick better than a porn star. I'd always been weak for a pretty face, and she had the pretty face and a banging body to match. I fucked her two days after first meeting. I thought it was going to be a one-time thing, but it ended up lasting for six whole months.

Janae had no clue that I was fucking another bitch because I hid it well. I never stopped loving her, fucking her, or spending time with her. I continued doing my same routine, and Janae never questioned anything that I did. As I stared down at her, I could see the pain in her eyes. This wasn't my first time cheating on her since she and I had gotten together. The first time was last year when my business started booming. I was tempted and ended up smashing one of my employees. I fired her ass after Janae found out about it because I knew Janae would never get back with me if the girl kept working with me. After I fired shorty, I begged Janae to come back to me. When she took me back, I promised myself I was never going to fuck around on Janae ever again.

I found myself in the same situation yet again, and I prayed that she took a nigga back. If I had to cut Lexi off, I was willing to do that shit because there was no way I was about to pick another bitch over Janae. Janae had been there when I didn't have shit, so no matter what, I wasn't about to leave her for another bitch who only was with me just for what I could give her.

Lexi had met me when I was successful and getting money, but I didn't know anything about the bitch's character to know whether she would hold me down like Janae had. Janae was one of a kind, and I didn't want to lose her.

"How could you hurt me like this?" Janae asked with anger in her voice.

"Baby, can we please go back to my place so we can talk. I don't want to talk to you outside like this."

"I'm not going anywhere with you. I don't even want to ride in the car with your lying ass."

I took a deep breath and let it out. I should have known that Janae was going to act like this. I didn't blame her. I would be acting the same way.

"Okay, fine. You ain't got to ride in my car. Can you just get your car and come over to my place so we can talk about our relationship?"

Janae held up her hand to stop me.

"I'm not going to your house either. Whatever you say, you can say it here."

After I seen that Janae wasn't going to change her mind, I eventually caved and tried to plead my case.

"Baby, I first want to tell you how sorry I am. I never meant to hurt you."

Janae folded her arms, and my heart skipped a beat.

"Do me a favor and don't lie to me. Because if you lie, it's only going to make me walk into my house, head toward my kitchen, grab my favorite butcher knife that I use to cut up your food with, and stab your ass in your heart for lying to me."

I took a deep breath because of how Janae stared at me. I didn't know if she was serious or not, and I wasn't trying to find out.

"I don't want to hear shit that you got to say. I just want answers."

"Baby, I'm willing to give you that."

"Don't call me baby because I'm not your baby. Matter fact, just shut the fuck up and let me talk."

I didn't bother speaking. Instead, I waited for her to speak.

"I've been there for you and have held your ass down from day one, and this is how you going to do me? I forgave you the first time you cheated on me, but I'm tired of this shit. How in the hell are you going to cheat on me with bitches who weren't down with you when you didn't have a dime in your damn pocket? Your dick shouldn't even get hard for another bitch. I'm going to keep it real with your ass. What I fucking did for you, for us, I deserved some fucking loyalty in return, but you ain't gave me that shit. This bitch had the nerve to call my fucking phone and curse me out about my own damn man. You were supposed to be home with me, but you out in the streets getting your dick wet instead."

"Can I talk now?"

"Yeah, you can talk, but don't dare lie to me."

"Janae, I love you with all my heart and soul. You know I appreciate everything that you have done for us. I never wanted to hurt you. Please forgive me. I'm going to stop fucking around with Lexi. I'm willing to do anything to keep you with me. I was just about to say more when Janae smacked me in the face. I wasn't expecting that shit because Janae had never laid her hands on me. I held on to my cheek as she began to curse me slam out.

"Nigga, keep your fucking sorry. I don't want to hear all them fucking lies. Nigga, you ain't sorry, because if you were, you would have never stuck your dick in that bitch in the first place. Maybe I could have looked past you fucking her one time, but no, you been fucking this bitch for six months. She calling my damn phone telling me to leave her man alone like you and her in a committed relationship. You didn't even tell the bitch you had someone. You told her you was single, and guess what? You are single."

I saw the tears falling from her eyes, and it broke my heart. I tried grabbing her, but she quickly snatched her arm away.

"Don't fucking touch me, Darnell. It all finally makes sense why your hoe ass didn't want to get us a place together. You out here fucking around on me and didn't want to get caught up."

Janae wiped the tears from her soft brown eyes before she stared back at me with pure hatred.

"No, that wasn't the reason why we didn't get our own place. Where was Princess going to go? You know that Princess and you split rent, and I figured you didn't want to up and leave her until the lease was up."

I must have said the wrong shit because Janae attacked my ass. I caught hell pulling her off of me. I pushed her up on my car and kept her pinned down until I felt like she wasn't going to attack me anymore.

"Let me fucking go!" Janae spat at me.

"I will let you go if you promise you won't attack me."

"Nigga, you ain't even worth it," Janae replied spitefully.

Damn, that shit really hurt, but I looked over it and told myself it was because she was just angry. I released her, and she quickly ran toward her front door to her apartment.

"Janae, I love you," I yelled out emotionally.

Janae looked back at me and shook her head.

"Darnell, there is no you and me. I'm done. I can't do this with you. I can't trust you anymore, and to be honest, we can't move forward if my trust is fucked up."

I wanted to run after her to hold her and tell her just how much I loved her, but as the door closed in my face, I realized that I had just lost the love of my life, and it wasn't any guarantee that she and I would ever try to make things work.

****

The Next Day

I had just left from checking up on my employees at Bustin' Bubbles and was heading to grab me some lunch from Arby's when my phone began to blast Migos. I groaned when I saw Lexi's name pop up. I had been avoiding her ass like the plague since Janae and I had gotten into it yesterday. I didn't have shit to say to her because I blamed her ass for even going through my phone and calling Janae in the first place. Now Janae didn't even want to speak to a nigga. I had tried calling and texting her all last night, and I got no answer. After a while, a nigga gave up. I caught the hint. She didn't want a nigga no more, but I could see the love in her eyes when she walked away from me yesterday. I was just going to give her some time to think and get her feelings in check before I hit her back up again. There was no way I was going to let Janae go.

I was just about to ignore Lexi's call but decided to answer because she was going to continue to blow my line up if I kept ignoring her.

"What you want, Lexi?" I mumbled into the phone.

"I like how you ignoring my ass. You and I have been fucking around for six months. How in the hell you just going to cut a bitch off like that?"

"Lexi, I was really feeling you until yesterday."

Lexi laughed into the phone like she was possessed.

"You didn't tell me that you had a bitch at home. I go through your phone and see all these text messages and phone calls to a bitch name Janae. How was I to damn know I was the side bitch?"

"You had no business going through my damn phone in the first place."

All I wanted to do was hurry off the phone so I could go home and go to sleep. I had too much on my damn mind to be fussing with a bitch who wasn't mine."

"If I would have known you had someone, I would have never fucked around with you."

I laughed because I knew Lexi was lying. She didn't give two fucks about me having a girl at home. All she saw was the money, and her ass was down to pop her pussy."

"Look, I think you and I need to talk in person about this issue," Lexi insisted

My head was telling me to not do that shit. *Just tell the bitch it was over with and disconnect the call. Change your number if you have to, but don't go to her spot.*

"Give me twenty minutes, and I will be pulling up at your spot."

"Cool," Lexi replied.

I disconnected the call as I switched lanes, turned on Pleasant Hill Road, and headed back toward Russell Parkway. Twenty minutes later, when I pulled up at Lexi's apartment, I said a silent prayer that nothing got out of hand. I didn't have the time or patience for Lexi to start acting a damn fool. Most niggas would have told her over the phone and blocked her ass if she kept blowing up their line, but I wasn't that type of nigga. I felt like she deserved for me to at least tell her face to face since I had fucked around with her for so long.

I was just about to knock on her door when it swung open. There stood Lexi looking sexy as hell. She was dressed in a pair of gray booty shorts, a black tank top, and a pair of black and gray Nike socks. She moved aside as I stepped into her tiny living room. I knew I had fucked up when she closed the door behind me and pushed me down on her black leather couch.

I stared at her body as she folded her arms over her plump titties. I could tell by her face that she was in her feelings about what we had discussed over the phone. Before she even opened her mouth, I beat her to it.

"The only reason why I came over here is because I owe you a personal apology. You and I been kicking it for a minute, but what you and I shared must come to an end. When you called my girl yesterday and told her all that bullshit, that really fucked everything up."

Lexi placed her hands on her hips while she stared at me.

"Nigga, do you think I give a fuck about you having a bitch?"

I shook my head because I already knew that Lexi didn't give a fuck if I had someone or not. She wasn't trying to be my girl; she just wanted to make sure her money was secure.

"I think you and I need to dead this shit. I want to do the right thing by my girl, and I can't do that shit if I'm still fucking around with you."

Lexi smirked before she walked over to where I was sitting and placed her juicy booty on my lap. She bent down and placed her soft lips on my mine. Her sweet perfume invaded my nose as our tongues danced with one another.

When she pulled away she whispered in my ear, "As long as you don't tell, I won't say nothing either."

My dick was on swole as she caressed it with her soft hands. As I closed my eyes, images of Janae began to surface. Her soft, milk chocolate skin, soft brown eyes, curvy figure, long hair, and pretty smile burned a hole in my mind. I pulled away and pushed Lexi off of me. I couldn't cheat on Janae. Lexi looked at me with a blank expression as I made my way to her front door.

“I can’t keep fucking around with you, Lexi. You going to get a nigga caught up.”

Lexi switched her ass over to where I was standing before she slid her tongue into my mouth. I wanted to push her ass off of me, but when she undid my belt buckle, unzipped my cargo pants, and got down on her knees, there was no coming back from that.

Lexi knew exactly what to do to make me forget what was really important, and that was Janae. As her lips wrapped around my dick, I pushed the images of Janae out of my mind. I moaned as she took my dick into her mouth and didn’t gag. I stared down at her as she made my dick disappear and reappear over and over again. This bitch had my toes curling as she popped my dick out her mouth, spit on it, and stroked me up and down before making my dick disappear in her mouth again.

I wrapped my hands in her hair as I pushed her head back and forth on my dick.

Damn, this bitch knew how to suck a dick. I pushed my dick down her throat one last time before I felt I was ready to cum. I yanked my dick out of her mouth one last time and painted her face with my cum.

Lexi wiped her face off as I bent her fine ass over the living room couch and began to tongue her juicy pussy down. I slid two fingers inside as I licked and sucked on her pussy from the back. The constant moaning of my name let a nigga know I was hitting the right spot. I played with her pussy until her legs began to shake, and she covered my tongue with her sweet nectar. I smacked her ass a few good times and watched it jiggle as I slid into her hot pussy.

I held her hips as I gave her some deep strokes while she screamed out my name and told me to fuck her harder. That was all I needed to hear before started slamming into her pussy over and over. Her pussy juices saturated my dick. I was giving her all the dick, and she was taking it like a pro. I smacked her ass before I gripped her weave and yanked her head back as I fucked her until she creamed on my dick. I slid out of her as I turned her over and slid between her legs. I kissed and sucked on her titties just before I slid my dick back inside her. I watched her facial expressions as I worked my dick in and out of her pussy. I took my free hand and played with her titties while she rubbed on her clit.

Sweat dripped from our bodies, but we continued to fuck until her legs began to shake and her loud screams invaded my ears. I slammed into her pussy a few more times just before I buried my cum deep inside her honey box. Lexi and I were both tired as hell from our love session. I watched her as she stood up a few moments later and began to get dressed. The whole time I put back on my clothes, I was trying to decide what was next. Should I continue to break Lexi off some of this good wood, or should I dead the relationship? After she and I were both dressed, she didn't hesitate to walk over to where I was standing and place a soft kiss on my lips before whispering in my ear, "I'm never letting you go."

Princess

As I stared at myself in the mirror, I noticed that my face had a glow to it that I hadn't seen since I was with my last boyfriend, Hakeem. Just thinking of Hakeem still brought tears to my eyes. I swear that nigga broke my heart and had fucked my mind up to the point of no return. I have always been the type of bitch to give my all, but Hakeem had played me like a little bitch. As I thought back to the day that our paths crossed, I couldn't help but cry.

I had just pulled a double shift, and I was tired as hell. It was close to 11:00 p.m. I was on way home when my tire blew out. I nearly killed myself as I swerved out of traffic and pulled over. I knew nothing about tires but was angry at myself because one of coworkers a few days prior had told me that my wire was showing in my front tire, and I needed to get a new tire. I brushed it off because I thought it wasn't that bad. Now, I was on side of the road with a blown-out tire and a dead cell phone sitting on the passenger seat. I thanked the man above that I didn't get hurt or hurt anyone in the process. Cars zoomed past me as I stepped out of my car and tried to see how bad the damage was. A few moments, later a car pulled over behind mine. I was grateful, but at the same time, I was ready to pepper spray who ever stepped out if they were on some bullshit.

A nigga stepped out, walked over to where I was standing, and asked if I needed any help. I held on to my pepper spray tightly in my right hand as he walked closer to me. When he got closer, I told him that my tire had blew out. He walked over to my car and shook his head before walking over to where I was standing.

"You lucky you didn't kill yourself."

"I know," I mumbled.

I tried not to stare, but I couldn't help it. The man who was standing before me had me mesmerized. He was tall, slim, and the complexion of a dark chocolate candy bar. He rocked a low fade, and his goatee was trimmed just like I liked. He was dressed in a polo shirt and a pair of black jeans. He must have noticed how I was staring because he quickly smiled and held out his hand.

"My name is Hakeem. What's yours?"

"I'm Princess," I choked out.

"Princess," he repeated. "That's a beautiful name."

"Thank you."

"Do you need a ride home?"

I looked up at him as I debated if I should tell him the truth. I looked back at my car and thought about my dead phone and thought the best way to get home was to ask him to take me.

"I don't have a way home," I told him truthfully.

Hakeem stared back at me as he rubbed his goatee.

"How about I give you a ride home?"

I agreed, and he got me home safely. As soon as he pulled up at my spot, he quickly asked for my number, and I gave it to him. From that day forward, we were inseparable.

I wiped the tears from my eyes because it was time that I moved on from Hakeem. He was nothing but a cheater and a liar. I always thought I would never be attracted to a nigga ever again until I laid eyes on Cameron's sexy ass. Even though I had only been texting and talking on the phone with Cameron for a week, I felt it in my soul that he was different. It was something about him that had my soul on fire every time I heard his voice. Right now I was on this high, and I didn't want to get off of it. I had just stepped out the shower so I could get ready for work when my phone began to blast Chris Brown's "On Me." My heart skipped a beat because I already knew who it was. As soon as I opened the text, my stomach fell to the floor.

Cameron: *I'm really feeling you Lil' Mama. Where you at? Let me come scoop you up.*

Me: *I'm home and I'm about to head to work.*

Cameron: *Damn, text me your address. I can come by and scoop you up and drop you off to work.*

As I stared down at the text, I bit my lip. Damn, my heart was telling me let him come by and scoop me up, but how was I going to get my black ass home later tonight? As soon as I asked myself that question, my phone lit up again.

Cameron: *I'm willing to scoop you up when you get off. Just let a nigga know your schedule.*

Me: *Okay cool. I got to be to work in another hour. I live at the Castaways Apt 290.*

Cameron: *On the way.*

I hurried to get dressed in my KFC uniform. The whole time I was putting on my eyeshadow and eyeliner, my hand shook. My nerves were on edge because this was going to be my first time seeing Cameron since I first met him. I had just put on my KFC hat when I heard a knock on my door. I stared at myself in the mirror one last time before I ran toward the door and opened it. My heart felt like it was about to jump out my chest when I saw Cameron standing on my doorstep dressed in a pair of black skinny jeans, a green and black pullover, and a pair of black boots. His dreads were pulled back in a ponytail, and he was rocking a black and green cap on his head. His diamonds glistened in his ear. This nigga was breathtaking and had a bitch weak in her knees. I had never been the type of bitch to be attracted to niggas like Cameron, but it was something about him that had a bitch drawn to him. I quickly grabbed my keys and locked up. As I followed him to 2018 black and silver, custom made Dodge Charger, I began to hate that Janae wasn't home to see him. Damn, she would have been speechless. Cameron was the type of nigga that Janae would have been attracted to. When this nigga opened my door for me, I almost died. Not only was he sexy as hell, but this nigga was a gentleman and knew how to treat a woman. I looked at him and then at the car in shock, and he must have seen my expression because he laughed.

"Just looking at your reaction is priceless."

"Was I that noticeable?"

"Yes, you were."

"I was just shocked. I didn't take you as a guy that would open doors for anyone."

His laughter filled the car and warmed my heart.

"You a queen. I will always give a queen this type of treatment."

I sat back in the seat and began to ponder what he meant by that statement. So was he saying that if I was a thot, I wouldn't get treated like a queen? I thought to myself. My thoughts went completely blank when he zoomed out of my complex and headed toward KFC on North Davis Drive. We talked and laughed for a few moments before I heard Chris Brown's "High End" in the background. I didn't hesitate to cut the volume up. Chris Brown blasted from the speakers as he weaved through traffic. When his hand caressed my thigh, I almost lost it. Just his touch was driving me up the wall. I was glad when he pulled up at KFC because I felt as if I was about to pass out if I didn't get some air. I tried to rush out the car, but he grabbed my hand to stop me.

"What time you want me to pick you up?"

I looked around as a few customers stared at us.

"I should be off by nine."

"Okay, cool, but before you go. I just want to tell you thank you for letting me take you to work. If you need me, call or text me."

When he smiled at me, my heart skipped a beat.

I slammed the door behind me and headed into work. As soon as I stepped in, I wanted to walk my ass right back out.

Dee, my shift leader, wasn't in a good mood and was already talking shit to some of my coworkers. When she spotted me, she directed her anger toward me. I said a silent prayer as I headed to the computer to clock myself in. I hadn't even stepped foot in the kitchen before she started talking about I was late. I bit my tongue as I started prepping the mashed potatoes and eventually, she took her ass in her office and slammed the door.

"I'm so tired of that bitch," Travis mumbled as he walked over to where I was making the mashed potatoes.

"I swear that bitch is crazy. She need a damn man."

"Don't no nigga got time for no bitch always talking shit. I know I don't want that shit."

Travis and a few other of our coworkers laughed.

I shook my head as I moved past him and started pouring the potatoes in the small styrofoam cups. I looked back at Travis and noticed that he wasn't doing shit but staring at my ass.

"Nigga, while you over there staring, you need to be helping me," I snapped at him.

"Damn, Princess, what's up with you?"

"Nothing is wrong with me. We got a lot of shit to do. We don't got time to be sitting around. I ain't got time to be hearing that bitch yelling about we behind."

Travis sighed before he finally started to help me with the mashed potatoes and gravy. I groaned when I heard Tonya screaming my name up front.

"Can you handle this by yourself?"

"Yes, Princess, I got this. Go see what Tonya ass want."

I nodded and ran up front to find that Tonya was behind and needed help packing. I got in position and started packing while she rung up the customers. I swear I worked two hours straight, and the line still wasn't letting up. I was tired as hell and was sweating like crazy, but there was no time to take a break. After the line had settled down, I headed toward the back when I ran into Nikki, who was complaining that they needed some slaw made up. I grabbed my jacket and headed toward the freezer where I began to make up the slaw. It was freezing in there, but I had to get the job done because no one ever wanted to make the coleslaw. I always was the one who had to make it up. I was in the middle of stirring the coleslaw when Dee's bitch ass came all the way in the freezer to start some mess with me.

At first, I tried to ignore her ass, but when the bitch got in my face, I nutted the fuck up on her.

"I know you hear me talking to you, Princess. Don't fucking ignore me. I've been looking for you. You need to get out front and ring some of them orders up. The lines are backed up."

"Dee, I can't go up front if we all out of coleslaw. Nobody want to make the coleslaw," I tried reasoning with her.

When she started cursing at me, I lost it quickly.

"Look, bitch, I'm so sick and tired of your ass talking to me any kind of way. Your bitch ass always got something to say. Why don't get your ass out there and help out front? Don't come at me when you know I'm the only one who makes the coleslaw. I'm only one person. What more do you want from me?"

"I want your ass to get off the clock!" she yelled at me.

A bitch was tired as hell, and I had worked seven hours straight with no break. She must have thought I was about to cry just because she told me to clock out. I stopped what I was doing and walked out that freezer as she followed me talking shit. If I wasn't scared to go to jail, I would've swung on the bitch. I had just clocked out when some of my coworkers were trying to figure out what had happened. The drive thru was deep as fuck, but I didn't give two fucks as I waved at my coworkers and dipped the fuck out. I pulled out my cell and dialed Cameron's number. He picked up on the first ring.

"I need for you to come get me."

"I'm on the way."

Five minutes later, I heard Migos' "Get Right Witcha" blasting before I saw Cameron pull up at KFC. All eyes were on me as I got my tired ass in the car.

"Damn, boo, what happened to you. You look like you been fighting."

He turned off Migos as he stared at me.

"Me and Dee got into it again. The bitch is lethal. I was very close to knocking the bitch out. She made me clock out."

Cameron shook his head as he zoomed out of KFC parking lot.

"I ain't trying to get all in your business, but I think you need to get you another job."

"Uh huh. I agree before I murder that bitch."

Cameron laughed, and I looked at him with the evil eye.

"What's so funny?"

"The fact you ain't nothing but five feet tall. Who you going to murder, though?"

I shook my head at his ass.

"Look, nigga, I will hurt that bitch."

"Oh, I believe you," he joked.

"I'm so ready to go home and take a long bath."

Cameron eyed me when he pulled up at the red light.

A few moments later, he pulled up at my complex, and I felt nothing but relief. I was just about to thank him for the ride when I noticed he was getting out the car with me. My keys jingled as I tried to find the right one to open my door. I wasn't expecting Cameron to follow me inside. I thought his ass was going to drop a bitch off, but he had other shit in mind. I pulled off my black KFC cap, shirt, and removed my pants right in the living room. I didn't give two fucks that Cameron was looking at me when I was half naked.

As I headed toward my bathroom, I could feel his eyes on my body, but he didn't run behind me or approach me. It was something about Cameron that had a bitch feeling shit that I had never felt before. When I was around him, I felt safe, and I trusted this nigga way too much to have just met him. Being around him made me feel relaxed, and his vibe was so soothing that I didn't feel alarmed walking around the house wearing nothing but my white tank top and a black pair of thongs. No words were spoken as I ran my bath water, removed my clothes, and slid into the hot bubble bath that I had ran for myself.

I was relaxing in the tub when I heard the sports channel playing.

Well, it looked like he was making himself at home while I soaked my day away. I closed my eyes as I tried to forget about the pissy job that I had probably lost. As the water caressed my tired body, I told myself that I didn't need that job anyway. I had some money in my savings to pay my half of the rent until I found another job. I was so into my thoughts that I didn't even hear Cameron come into the bathroom with me. I gasped when his hands touched my neck.

"Relax, it's just me," he whispered in my ear.

I sat back for a moment and moaned when he began to rub my neck and shoulders as he talked gently into my ear.

"I know things been crazy lately, but I want you to know that I'm here for you if you ever need me. I don't know what you have done to me, but it's something about you that got a nigga wanting to get to know you."

Cameron was taking the very thoughts from my brain. I was questioning the same things. I wondered if he felt the same connection that I did.

"I respect you, and I would never do no foul shit to disrespect you in any way. You different from the average chick I been with. I want to get to know you better. How do feel about that?"

I turned around making sure to keep my titties covered as I stared into his soft brown eyes.

"I would love to get to know about you better also." My heart skipped a beat as I felt butterflies in my stomach. His cologne tickled my nose as he leaned over me to let my bath water out.

I waited until he stood up and closed the door behind himself before I stood up and began to dry my body off. I wrapped my body in a plush blue towel and stepped into my room to find Cameron sitting on my bed holding a bottle of my favorite coconut oil.

"Bring your ass over here and lay down. I'm about to work some magic on you."

I tiptoed over to my bed and held onto my towel as I laid down on my stomach.

"I'm going to give you a nice massage. You think you can handle that?"

I laughed before telling him that I could.

When he slid down my towel, my pussy began to drip with anticipation.

Bitch, you better calm your ass down. You only getting a massage.

I closed my eyes as he poured the lukewarm coconut oil over my back and began to rub me down.

He quickly turned away as I slid off the bed. I was just about to head to my closet to find something to wear when his phone began to blast Gucci Mane. His facial expression changed, and I knew instantly that the phone call must have been important.

He turned away from me, and I took the hint that he didn't want me to know who he was talking to.

I grabbed a shirt and a pair of leggings out of my walk-in closet, but I strained my ear to try to listen to who he was talking to.

When he told the person on the phone that he was coming home soon and that he loved them, I knew instantly that it was another bitch he was talking to. My heart felt as if it had been ripped out my chest. I should have known that this nigga probably had a bitch already. This nigga was too damn sexy to be damn single, but that wasn't why I was upset. I was upset that I finally had a desire to be with a nigga, and he already had a bitch. I don't know why I was all in my damn feelings when I didn't even ask this nigga when he first asked for my number if he was single or not. I wanted to cry because the one man I felt something for was already committed. But instead of crying like a little bitch, I finished putting my clothes on before I stepped out my closet like I didn't give two fucks. All the chemistry that I felt before was dead and gone.

He stared at me and licked his lips, but I ignored the shit. He walked over to me, and his cologne invaded my nose.

"I enjoyed spending time with you. I hope you and I can get together again."

I took a step back and folded my arms.

"I don't think that will be necessary. I think you need to gone and get back home to your girl. I don't play second to no bitch."

Cameron looked at me for a moment before he shook his head. I stared at him and didn't dare look away.

"I'm going to keep it real with you, Princess. I ain't going to lie. Yes, I got a girl at home, but it's just something about you that I can't shake. I feel so connected to you, and you can't stand here and act like you don't feel it too. I just want to be present in your life and just get to know you better. I ain't trying to fuck if that's what you worried about."

I unfolded my arms and took a few steps toward him. I stared up at him, and I swear I felt the same chemistry yet again. I was letting down my guard with him, but it felt so right. When his hands began to caress my cheek, I felt goosebumps cover my body.

"There's something about you."

I nodded my head because I agreed.

My heart began to pound against my chest when he looked down at me and tried to kiss me on my lips. I pulled away and he ended up kissing me on my cheek.

"Like I said before, I don't come second to no bitch."

Cameron chuckled.

"You got me going crazy about you, lil' mama. Can you at least be a nigga's friend?"

"Of course," I choked out.

He smiled before grabbing my hand and placing a kiss on it.

My heart fluttered as he walked past me and headed out my front door. I followed him and watched him as he hopped into his car and headed out.

Cameron

As soon as I pulled up at the traffic light, I quickly lit the blunt that I had just rolled. So much shit was on my mind that I needed something to keep a nigga calm. Since I had met Princess, she had been invading a nigga's mind. It was something about her that had a nigga feeling some type of way. I had never felt this type of connection with any female, but it was something about her that was different. I felt guilty as hell because I had been over chilling with Princess part of the day and hadn't even been home with my own girl. When she called me, I heard the concern in her voice, but I pushed the guilty feelings far away from my heart and told her that I had gotten caught up with some shit at the trap house. Brianna knew what type of lifestyle I lived, so she believed that shit. Ten minutes later, when I pulled up to my spot, I sat in the car and rolled me one last blunt and rolled my window down to let some of the smoke out.

As the smoke burned my eyes, I couldn't help but think about Princess. Damn, I was tempted to kiss her sexy lips, but when she pulled away, I knew I was moving too quickly for her. If she would have been any other bitch, her ass would have gotten fucked today, but I had respect for her ass because I knew she wasn't like them other hoes. When I did give her the dick, I knew she was going to be crazy about a nigga. I could see the lust in her eyes today, but I felt good that she and I both didn't act on any of that shit. There was no way I wanted to break Brianna's heart. At the end of the day, she had held a nigga down when none of these other bitches were even down with the shit. Whatever Princess and I had going on was going to have to wait. If she and I were going to be together, I knew that we would be, but right now, I was going to do the right thing and love the girl I already had at home.

After I had finished smoking my blunt, I headed into my apartment, and Brianna was nowhere to be found. I headed to my bedroom and stood in the doorway. I watched Brianna play in her pussy as she laid on her back in our bed. I licked my lips as I pulled off my jacket and walked over to where she was softly moaning. I slid between her legs and pushed her hand away from her honey box and replaced it with my tongue. She moaned my name as I began to lick up her juices.

Damn, she had a nigga feeling guilty as hell. I had never not been around to please my girl. I was lusting over Princess's pussy when I had Brianna sitting home craving some of this good wood. When her legs began to shake and her pussy quivered, I knew she was about to milk my tongue. After I licked up her cum, I placed sweet kisses up her stomach toward her nipples and began to suck on each one before I pulled my dick out my pants. I was ready to get inside her pussy and wasn't bothered by not getting head from her. I slid between her legs and entered her with one slow push.

She immediately wrapped her legs around my waist and cried out my name as I began to beat her pussy up. Her pussy was dripping wet, and I was tearing her walls up. She wrapped her hands in my dreads as I gave her some deep, long strokes that made her cry out each time I moved in and out of her.

"Fuck this pussy!" Brianna screamed out.

Damn, I loved when her ass told me some shit like that. I pulled out of her and slammed into her a few more times before I flipped her over and arched her back as I began to fuck her from the back. I smacked her ass as I drilled my dick in and out of her kitty kat. I moaned when I saw her cream over my dick. I kissed her on her neck and played with her titties as I rammed my dick into her a few more times.

"Oh, shit," Brianna cried as I held on to her hips as she met each thrust that I was sending her way.

I pulled out of her only for her to turn around and begin to suck on my dick. I closed my eyes as I wrapped my hands into her hair and moved her head back and forth as she sucked me off. I pushed my dick farther into her mouth until I heard her gag, and that's when I pulled back out. She held on to me as she sucked and stroked on my dick. I groaned when she pulled my dick out her mouth and began to lick my balls as she stroked my dick with her spare hand.

"Shit," I moaned.

I pulled my dick out her mouth as I stood up from the bed and picked her slim ass up.

I looked into her eyes as I pushed her ass up against the wall and began to bounce her up and down on my dick.

Her loud screams had a nigga weak as hell and had me ready to bust my nut all up in her pussy.

"I'm about to cum!" she screamed out.

When her body began to shake and I felt her hot liquid on my dick, I busted right after her.

We were both tired as hell and eventually made it back to the bed and laid down. I had fucked Brianna to sleep, and as she laid there with her eyes closed, I couldn't help but admire her beauty. She was honey brown, medium height, had a small waist but a fat ass, and full puffy lips that I loved kissing on. Brianna was sexy as hell, and her pussy was always on point. I kissed her gently on her lips and smiled when she mumbled something in her sleep.

I slid off the bed and headed straight to the shower. As the hot water began to beat down on my body, I closed my eyes and wasn't surprised to see Princess staring back at me. Just when I thought I had gotten her out of my mind, here she was invading my head space. Even though I had just gotten some A1 pussy, my dick still got hard as hell as I thought about Princess. I moaned quietly as I began to stroke myself a few times before I went in for the kill. Damn, I hated to masturbate when I had just busted a fat ass nut, but Princess had a nigga wanting to slide up in her pussy. I squeezed my eyes shut as the water splashed over my face. I thought about Princess and how it would feel if I could get between her legs. I groaned as I thought about Princess riding my face, and that's when I caught my second nut. I shook my head as I started to wash myself clean after I was done, I stepped out the shower to find Brianna standing there with her hands folded over her chest.

"Who the fuck is Princess?"

I stood there not able to speak, but I had no idea what to tell her. Brianna smiled evilly before she walked away from me. My heart pounded because I didn't know what had just happened. I was thinking that Brianna was going to get all up in my face and want to fight about me masturbating and moaning another girl's name, but she had done the complete opposite. I didn't know if I should be scared or grateful. Only time would tell.

*****

TWO WEEKS LATER

For two weeks straight, I took Princess to work and picked her back up. I didn't mind because I wanted to do anything to get closer to her. On the days that she had a fucked-up day, I always treated her to dinner with a back and foot massage. Finally, she was getting the day off, so I decided to scoop her fine ass up and take her out.

When I pulled up at her complex, she was already waiting for me outside. She was dressed in a gray spandex sweater that hugged her titties and a pair of black leggings with some gray snow boots. She had her hair pulled back in a bun and she was wearing very little makeup. My dick got on hard as I glared at her sexy ass. I stepped out my car and opened her door like the gentleman that I was. I zoomed out the complex before I looked over at her and noticed she was nodding her head to "Saturday Night" by 2 Chainz. I turned the music down and asked her where she wanted to go. Her eyes glowed when she told me that she wanted to hit the mall up.

I turned the music back up as I headed toward Watson Boulevard. The mall was packed as usual, so I ended up having to park at Sears and walking into the mall through their store. As soon as we stepped into the mall, Princess grabbed my hand and pulled me into Victoria's Secret. I watched her as she looked through some of their sexy lingerie. I had a hard time keeping my dick off hard every time she showed me something sexy that she was thinking about getting. Twenty minutes later, she had her hands full with all types of perfume and over five different pieces of sexy lingerie that had a nigga wanting to bend her ass over right then and give her pussy a pounding. When she looked down at my semi-hard dick, she smirked before she walked over to where I was posted up and whispered in my ear.

"Just think. If you was single, this pussy would be all yours."

Princess had a nigga speechless and had me ready to kick Brianna in the wind. When Princess pushed up on me and rubbed her spare hand over my dick, a nigga didn't hesitate to grab her ass and push her up against the wall. The store clerk was too busy talking on the phone to pay us any attention. I stared into her eyes as I pushed my hard dick against her.

"Lil' mama, don't play with me because I will fuck you."

Princess's eyes twinkled as she licked her juicy lips and had the nerve to wrap her legs around my waist.

I placed my lips on her neck and kissed on her as she moaned my name. I was close to kissing her lips when my phone began to blast Migos. I groaned with irritation when Princess and I pulled away from each other. When I noticed it was Icey J, I immediately picked up.

"Cameron, where you at, nigga? Some shit just went down. The trap house is surrounded with nothing but cops and the Feds. J Boy just called and told me that they looking for us."

I never thought that I was going to get caught up this early in the game. I had never been hot on the police or Feds' radar, so that only meant one thing. Someone had snitched and had sold some information to the cops. All I could think about was fucking somebody up.

"Wherever you at, you need to stay off the roads because I hear the helicopters."

"Where the fuck you at?"

"I'm hiding out at my girl's house."

"Ok, cool."

After we disconnected the call, I slid the phone back in my pocket. I walked over to where Princess was standing and told her we had to dip out. She looked at me with confusion, and I pulled her ass toward the cash register and threw the cashier some money and practically dragged Princess out the store.

"What the fuck wrong with you?"

"Feds and the cops out. They looking for me and my partner. I got to get the fuck out of sight for a minute."

I could see the fear in her eyes, and I knew then that Princess wasn't the type of female who was about that life. She was the type that dated niggas who had a clean background and fucked around with niggas with degrees and shit. She and I were opposites, but the feeling she gave me wouldn't go away. I pulled her by the hand as we worked our way through the crowded mall back to the car. I zoomed out the parking lot and was heading straight to her house to drop her off. I wanted to call Brianna to see had the cops been over to the place but decided to wait until I had Princess out the car. When I pulled up at Princess's spot, she looked back at me with sadness and worry in her eyes.

"Are you going to be okay?"

"Of course. I'm a street nigga. Fuck the Feds."

Princess still didn't get out the car. Instead, she looked at me and back at her apartment.

"You can stay at my place for a while. I don't live by myself, but my roommate won't mind. I don't think it's wise for you to go back to your place."

"I'm good, lil' mama. Cops don't know where I live. If they did, they already would be there, and my girl would have called me."

Princess nodded her head. She was just about to step out the car when I pulled her by her arm.

"I enjoyed the day with you."

I could tell by how she was looking that she wanted to cry.

"I will hit you up when shit cool down."

"Of course you will," Princess mumbled before slamming the car door and running toward her apartment.

As soon as I pulled out of Princess's complex, I pulled out my phone to hit Brianna up. I called her twice, but she didn't answer neither time. I called one last time only to have my call sent straight to voicemail. Something wasn't right. Brianna never missed my calls, and if she did, she always would text a nigga back. As I got closer to the apartment that Brianna and I shared, I got a feeling that something wasn't right, but I ignored it. I pulled up at my spot and hopped out. I was just about to open the door when it swung open. Brianna was standing there looking good as hell.

She was rocking a pair of navy blue booty shorts and a white top with her hair pulled up in a high ponytail. Her honey brown skin was lightly covered in makeup, and her lips were popping with her glistening lip gloss. She stepped aside to let me in, and I immediately asked her if she had seen the cops or Feds. She shook her head at me and stared at me like I was crazy.

"What's up with you? Why you asking me about the Feds?"

"My partner just called and told me that the Feds and cops are out looking for us. Somebody done snitched. The cops at the trap house asking people questions and shit."

She was just about to speak when a loud knock came at the door. She looked at me, and I looked at her.

When I took a peek outside, I noticed the police and Feds were waiting outside. Them bastards had cut their sirens off to make sure we didn't hear their ass coming.

I was ready to run, but Brianna stopped me.

She kissed me lightly on my lips before telling me to be quiet, and she would handle it.

A voice in my head told me to get the fuck out of there, but my heart told me that Brianna had my back. Just when Brianna disappeared around the corner, the Feds and cops busted open the back door and came right on in. I was cornered, and I had no place to hide.

"Police! You're under arrest!" the cops screamed in union.

I didn't give a fuck about the police. All I cared about was the safety of my girl, Brianna.

"Brianna!" I yelled out her name.

A few moments later, she appeared, and my heart dropped when I heard one of the Feds giving her praise on how well she had done. Tears stung my eyes as one of the agents walked over to where she was posted up at and placed his lips on hers. I looked away as the police officer came behind me and placed the cuffs on my hands.

I was hurt and angry that I had let that bitch play me. I had no clue that the bitch was an undercover cop. She had hid the shit so well. As I slid into the back seat of the police car, I began to have flashbacks of the times that Brianna was always eager to help a nigga out. I never thought anything of it. She had me believing that she was riding for me the whole time, but really, she was investigating me. I was never the type of nigga to cry, but

I couldn't stop the few tears from falling from my eyes. There was no way I was ever going to trust another bitch again.

JANAE

The next day

Today, I was off, so I decided today would be the perfect day to clean up. I slid out of my bed and hopped in the shower. As the water caressed my face and body, tears began to fall from my eyes. I still couldn't stop crying about how shit had went down with Darnell. Even though he had been calling and texting me nonstop, I still didn't respond back to him. I just couldn't risk talking to him. I didn't want him to know the effect that he had on me. I didn't want him to know that I was barely able to function at work or even get out of bed in the mornings. I was putting up a front to everyone that I was okay, but deep down inside, I missed my nigga.

Why couldn't he love me and be a good ass nigga? Why did he have to lie and cheat on me with another bitch? I asked myself as I wiped the tears from my eyes. After I had cried my eyes out in the shower, I stepped out and wrapped a towel around my body and headed in my bedroom where I searched throughout my closet for something to wear.

I decided on a pair of black leggings, a hot pink top, and a pair of hot pink socks. I pulled my hair up into a high bun and slid on my black house shoes before I started to clean up. I had just made up my bed and started folding up the clothes that were piled on the floor when I ran across the gold chain that Darnell had given me for my birthday last year. I had been looking for that necklace for over a week but couldn't find it.

How in the hell did you end up in my clothes? I touched the locket with my hands before tears began to fall from my eyes yet again. I closed my eyes as I began to think about the day he had given me this necklace. The love that we had back then was real.

Even though it was my birthday, I woke up in a bad mood because I had to work. There was no way that I couldn't show up because we were short staffed. Everyone thought waiting tables was easy, but the shit was hard as hell when people were constantly coming to eat all day. I had slaved my ass off all that week. I expected them to let me have this one day off, but it was denied. I turned around from getting dressed and noticed Darnell was laid up in bed sleeping peacefully. I wanted so badly to take my frustration out on him. The fact that he didn't wake me and tell me happy birthday had my ass fired up. I had just gotten through putting on my lip gloss and was about to start on my hair when Darnell stood up, walked over to me, and placed a kiss on my cheek before rubbing his hands up and down my tense body.

All the anger and frustration that I felt evaporated, and he was all I cared about. He turned me around as I faced the mirror and placed the gold chain around my neck.

I opened the locket, and tears fell from my eyes as I read what was engraved inside.

"My heart beats for your love." On the left side of the locket was a picture of him and I together.

I turned toward him as he wrapped me in his arms and kissed me on my lips. When he slid his tongue into my mouth, my knees went weak.

"I know you upset you got to go to work, but just know when you get home tonight, I'm going to make you feel real good."

I just wished that Darnell and I could go back to the old times when our love could withstand anything. I placed the necklace in my jewelry box where it belonged. After over an hour of separating my clothes and cleaning up my room, I finally laid my ass back down. I was tired as hell. I was just about to close my eyes when my phone went off, and I saw Princess's name pop up on my screen.

"What up boo?"

Hearing Princess crying made me sit up in bed and pull the phone from my ear. It was one in the afternoon, and Princess was at work. Princess never called me

…ad just happened. It

…ith her job. I was sick and

…I swear, if it was about

…ar and make a trip to

…Why you crying?"

…one that Cameron is

…ecause Princess and

…ether over the past two

…going on because Princess

…e she got rid of Hakeem's

…s all sad and depressed, so

… up on game.

"You like him, Princess?"

"Yes," Princess cried into the phone.

I became quiet as I tried my best to calm her down.

"Princess, you know I love you like a sister, and I want you to be happy. I hate to see you hurting and crying like you are, but I'm going to keep it real with you. If you want to be with Cameron, then him getting locked up is something that you going to have to deal with. You got to be strong enough to keep your mind and heart stable. You can't be flipping out the bag sweetie. This is what comes with dating a street nigga. You know you have wiped my tears plenty of times when my boyfriends would get those thirty days in the county jail back in the day."

Princess laughed.

She and I both knew that all I ever dated were pure savages. My boyfriends stayed locked up more than they stayed out with me. Princess never dated a street nigga, so this was all new to her.

"Princess, you going to get through this."

When Princess finished crying, I felt so much better. She had me on edge when she cried because Princess was stronger than that shit. She rarely cried, so when she mentioned that her tears were for Cameron, I knew instantly that Princess was already in too deep.

Dating a street nigga wasn't for everyone. I prayed that Princess knew what she was getting herself into, and I prayed this Cameron nigga wasn't playing any games because if he was, I sure hated to be him. Princess was the nicest bitch that you could know, but if you got on her bad side and pushed her too hard, that's when the beast would come out of her.

I could remember the first time that Princess had ever fallen in love back in high school. When rumors started circulating that her man was taking another bitch to prom, Princess confronted the nigga about it. Of course, he denied it. Lord, why did he do that? When it was time for prom and he didn't show up to take her, Princess nutted up. I had never seen her that angry. Back then, we didn't have a car, so we got one of our neighbors to drop us off at the high school instead. When we stepped in the prom, we spotted her boyfriend, Nick. He was so busy feeling up on the same bitch he denied that he didn't even notice Princess was watching him. Princess didn't give two fucks or think twice as she snatched the bitch off of Nick and poured punch in his face. Nick had the nerve to try to talk shit to Princess and called her out her name a few times. Lord, why he do that? Princess didn't think twice about punching his ass. She punched his ass so hard that he fell back and broke the table. The bitch who was brave enough to even show up at the prom had the nerve to come at Princess like she wanted to fight. Princess didn't show the bitch any mercy. She nearly broke the girl's collar bone. I had to get her ass off that poor girl.

Like I said before, Princess was sweet, but don't fuck with her heart. When Hakeem broke her heart, I was shocked that she didn't try to murk that nigga. Maybe she didn't love him as much as she thought she did. I was the one who wanted to hurt his gay ass because I was tired of niggas doing my girl dirty.

Cameron was all over the news. The Feds raided his trap house according to what the news app just sent to my phone.

"Damn."

"What?" Princess asked with worry in her voice.

There was no way I wanted to tell Princess that Cameron was probably going to do some serious time if the Feds had raided him. He must have been under investigation for a hot minute.

"Janae, be real with me. Tell me what you thinking."

I sighed and told her the truth.

"Princess, I want to let you know that Cameron in some serious shit if the Feds raided his trap house. He might not be able to get himself out of this situation as quick as you think. It's probably going to be a minute before you hear anything. I just want you to remember that. I don't want you to be waiting by the phone thinking you going to hear from him right now."

Princess didn't speak for the longest moment. At first, I thought she had hung up.

"Princess, you still there?"

"Yes, I'm here. Janae, I never felt this way about no man. This feeling that I feel inside is so strong, and I don't know what to do about it. Never in my life have I ever felt like this with anyone. I know in my heart that Cameron is supposed to be my man."

I listened to her and didn't interrupt. My mind was racing a mile a minute as I absorbed everything she was telling me. I knew instantly that Princess was deeply infatuated with a bad boy. I just prayed he didn't break her heart.

****

I had just pulled up at my job when my phone began to vibrate. I groaned when I saw Darnell's name pop up on my screen. I quickly sent his ass to voicemail and headed into Cracker Barrel. I had just clocked in and was serving food when I heard someone call my name. I froze because I knew exactly who it was even before I turned around. My heart began to pound against my chest as I closed my eyes and tried my best to gain my composure. *I need to keep my emotions in check,* I kept telling myself.

I slowly turned around, and that's when I saw him. He was dressed in a pair of skinny jeans, a black and gray long sleeved thermal, and a pair of his black and gray Jordans. His silver and gold-plated grill gleamed in the light as he smiled at me. I felt butterflies in my stomach as he walked over to where I was standing.

"What are you doing here?" I asked with attitude.

"You gave me no choice. You wouldn't pick up none of my phone calls or text messages."

"That should have told you that I didn't want to see or talk to your ass."

"Baby, it's been two weeks. Are you really going to keep ignoring me?"

"Of course I am. Now, will you please leave? I'm at work."

Darnell didn't budge, so I took that time to try to walk off, but he quickly grabbed me by my arm.

"Can you please give me ten minutes of your time?"

A few of my coworkers looked at us, and I could see the lust in their eyes. A blind bitch could see that Darnell was sexy as hell. His dark chocolate skin, long dreads, nose ring, and grill had bitches going crazy over him.

I was just about to turn his ass down when my boss came from the back and told me that if it was important, then I had twenty minutes before I had to get back to work. I wanted to tell her I was good and nothing was wrong, but she quickly grabbed the dirty plates that I had in my hand and headed toward the kitchen.

Instead of fussing and fighting with him, I took him by the hand and told him to follow me. I headed toward the breakroom and closed the door behind us. I folded my arms as I stared up at him.

"Baby, I'm so sorry for everything I did. I promise you that I will never hurt you ever again. Please, just take me back. I'm not able to function without you."

"You look fine to me," I mumbled.

Darnell shook his head as he walked over to me. He tried to touch me, but I pulled away from him.

"You cheated on me, Darnell, with another bitch for over six months. I can't come back from that shit."

"Baby, please. I'm not talking to her no more. I want you. You the only woman I love. You and I have gone through so much together and have accomplished a lot. Why give all that shit up?"

"Because you was unfaithful twice, nigga. I'm good."

When Darnell got down on his knees and held on to my hips, I knew this nigga was serious about his feelings.

I had never seen Darnell like this since he and I had been together. My heart broke when he began to cry.

"Baby, please, take me back this last time. I promise I will never break your heart ever again."

"Nigga, get your ass off the floor."

He got off the floor and dusted himself off before I wrapped my arms around him. He lifted me up and placed a kiss on my neck. He sat me on top of the counter and slid between my legs as his lips met mine. His cologne invaded my nose, and I took his scent in. Damn, he was looking and smelling so good that I couldn't resist him. When he began to kiss and suck on my neck, it was game over. I moaned his name gently as he began to play with my titties.

"I've missed you so damn much. I want to show you just how sorry I am," he whispered in my ear.

He pulled away from me for a brief moment as he stared into my eyes.

"I love you, Janae. You're the only woman who has my heart. I belong to you, no one else."

I was just about to speak, but he stopped me when he placed his finger over my lips. All the anger I was feeling had evaporated, and all I felt was love. He held me tightly as our tongues danced with one another. We pulled away when we heard someone trying to come into the break room. He and I looked at one another before I jumped off the counter and opened the door for my coworker. She looked us up and down before walking past me. I grabbed Darnell's hand and walked him toward the front of the restaurant. He looked back at me one last time before placing one last kiss on my lips.

As I watched him leave, my heart began to ache for his touch. I just prayed that I had made the right decision with taking Darnell back. I had been fighting the decision for two weeks, but today was my breaking point. As soon as his lips met mine, I knew that I was fucked up from thinking clearly. I just hoped that this time Darnell had changed and was ready to be a better man because if he wasn't, I didn't know what I was going to do.

Darnell

You just don't know how relieved a nigga was feeling when I heard Janae tell me that she was willing to take a nigga back. I mean, she had a nigga scared for a minute. She had never just ignored a nigga for two weeks straight. I thought I had lost her for a minute. I wanted to do right by her. I truly loved her ass, but I also had an addiction to pussy and didn't know what to do about it. My heart belonged to Janae, but I just wished I could control the urges and leave Lexi's ass alone.

I was just about to head to my place when my phone began to vibrate. I looked down and noticed that it was Lexi texting me. I slid open the message and read it to myself. She wanted me to come over. I looked at my rearview mirror to make sure I could get over. When I found it was clear, I got in the other lane and headed toward Moody Road so I could go see what Lexi wanted. I was still on that high of finally getting Janae back in my life, and here was Lexi tempting me yet again.

Soon as I pulled up at her spot, I hopped out and knocked on her door. As soon as the door opened, she pulled me in and closed the door behind her.

"What's up with you?" I asked her as I stared at her half naked body.

Lexi licked her lips as she walked over to where I was standing and began to rub her hands over my lips and cheeks.

"I need a favor from you."

"What you need?" I asked her as I eyed her up.

She was dressed in a black thong with a black push up bra.

"I need some money to pay my rent."

"You know I got you."

Lexi licked her lips and my dick tingled. Damn, I couldn't stop thinking about her ass sucking on my dick.

"I've missed you, sexy daddy. I haven't heard nothing from you all day."

"Lexi, me and Janae got back together today."

Lexi was quiet for a minute and pulled away from me. Her round ass jiggled from side to side as she walked away from me. She turned back around and placed her arms over her chest.

"So, I guess you wanted to tell me that you and I are over with."

If I had it my way, I would love to keep them both, but I knew that wasn't going to be possible.

"Lexi, you fine and all, but I think it's best if you and I dead this shit."

I saw the hurt in her eyes, and I quickly dug out my wallet and passed her close to $5,000.

"Here's some money to pay your rent up for a few months."

Lexi took the money and placed it on her coffee table. When she brushed her ass up against my dick, I lost the last bit of restraint that I had.

I watched as Lexi got on her knees and pulled down my jeans and boxers and began to suck a nigga off. This was going to be the last time that I was going around with Lexi, so I was going to enjoy my damn self. I grabbed her by her hair and stuck my dick in her mouth. I moaned as she began to suck and slurp on my rock-hard dick.

"Damn, baby, suck this dick," I cried out as she began to deep throat a nigga. I pulled her off me a few moments later and bent her over her couch before I began to lick and suck on her pussy from the back. After she was good and wet, I slid my dick in and began to beat her pussy down. Her screams and crying only made me pound the pussy harder. I gripped her hips as I slammed into her over and over again until her legs began to shake, and she began to cream on my dick. A few moments later, I pulled out and slid between her thighs. I looked into her eyes as I played with her titties and hit her from the front. I was getting ready to bust my nut when she wrapped her legs around me and told me to fuck her harder. I gripped her by her hair as I slammed into her pussy a few more times before I busted my nut inside her juicy pussy.

She and I were both exhausted after our sex session. I slid my clothes back on as I watched her sexy ass count the money that I had passed her earlier. After she was finished counting the money, she walked over to where I was sitting, took a seat on my lap, and kissed me on my lips.

"I'm going to miss you, sexy daddy."

"I'm going to miss you too, boo, but I can't keep fucking around with you."

Even though I could see the hurt in Lexi's eyes, she didn't beg a nigga to stay, and I respected that shit because that was only going to make shit harder for me.

I kissed her for the last time before I walked out her door.

****

A FEW DAYS LATER

I had just left the grocery store and was on my way back to my place when I pulled out my cell and dialed Janae's number. My heart began to flutter when I heard her sexy voice in my ear.

"Hey, baby, you up yet?"

"Now I am." She chuckled sleepily into the phone.

"I was calling to see if you wanted to come over to my place later today so you and I can talk about us. We ain't really had time to talk about us."

"I know. I've been working double shifts this week."

"I understand."

We talked for a little while longer before I told her I would see her later. When I pulled up at my spot, I hopped out, and grabbed the few groceries that were in the back seat.

My plans for the night was to cook my girl a nice dinner and give her some much-needed loving. I had just stepped in the house and was about to start cooking when my phone began to vibrate. I groaned when I looked down at the screen and noticed that it was Lexi sending me a picture message. I waited for the picture to come through before I clicked on it. When my eyes saw the picture, I wished that I had forgotten what I had seen.

She had sent me a picture of her pretty little pussy with the caption that read *she missing your dick.* I was debating if I wanted to hop in my car, ride over there, and beat that pussy up. Instead of thinking with my dick, I decided, for once, to think with my head. My head was telling me to stay my ass home and cook Janae her dinner because if I played my cards right, Janae was going to give up the pussy anyway.

After I had unpacked the food, I quickly headed toward the bathroom so I could shower and get dressed for later that day. I decided to put on a black t-shirt with a pair of my gray sweatpants and my Nike sandals. I watched a little TV until the clock struck six, and I headed into the kitchen to put on the food. I had brought some ground beef, soft and hard taco shells, lettuce, and tomatoes. Tacos were Janae's favorite food. As I cooked the ground beef, I shot Janae a text message to let her know to come over in another hour. She replied that she was already on her way.

My heart was filled with joy knowing that Janae and I were finally about to spend some one on one time together. I just finished cooking the ground beef and was about to add the taco seasoning when I heard her knocking at my door. I stopped what I was doing and headed to the living room so I could let her in. When I opened the door, I embraced my baby before taking her hand and pulling into the kitchen.

"Damn, it smells good as hell in here. I can't believe you actually cooking."

I chuckled because I never cooked, but tonight was going to be special. I was willing to do whatever I had to, to make my baby feel good. A few moments later, we were eating, laughing, and talking about old times. As she sipped her wine, I sipped on my beer and watched her as she began to fidget in her seat. I knew her well, so I already knew she was nervous. I sat my beer down and cleared my throat so I could have her undivided attention. Our eyes connected, and I felt the love that she had radiating off her body.

My baby looked sexy as hell. She was dressed in a pair of blue jean leggings, a black long sleeve shirt, and a pair of black ankle boots. Her hair was bone straight, her lips were moisturized, and her chocolate complexion seemed to glow. I grabbed her hand from across the table as I began to tell her what was on my mind and in my heart.

"Janae, I know I have done a lot of shit that would make you want to walk out on me and never talk to me again, but I'm telling you the truth when I say that I love with all my heart and soul. You have stuck by me through thick and thin. You have helped me to better myself more than anyone ever has. You have taken so many risks for me, and I appreciate everything that you have done and everything you will do in the future. I love you, Janae. I just want you to know that no matter what happens between us, I will never stop loving you. I know I have hurt you and broke your heart. Please, I beg you to give me a chance to prove to you that my love for you is, in fact, real. Don't walk out on me. I'm willing to wait for however long it takes for you to trust me again with your heart."

I kissed her gently on both of her hands. Tears fell from her eyes, and my heart stung. If Janae had changed her mind about taking me back, I swear I was going to lose my mind and wasn't going to be able to function. Even though I had a lustful spirit that seemed to follow me around every day, Janae still had my soul in her hands. If she told me that she didn't love me and didn't want to be with me, then I wouldn't know how to cope with the rest of my life knowing she wasn't going to be present.

Janae wiped her tears and cleared her throat as she pulled her hands away from mine.

"I just want to say that you truly hurt me, Darnell. I loved you so damn much. Words can't describe the love I have for you, and to find that you had betrayed me yet again is heartbreaking. I don't want to lose you, but can I really lose someone who really isn't mine?"

I stood up, walked over to where she was sitting, bent down on one knee, and caressed her thigh with my hand.

"Baby, I don't belong to no one but you. Believe that."

Janae looked at me, and I saw the doubt in her eyes. I wanted to do everything in my power to change how she felt. I stood up and grabbed her by the hand as I pulled her to the bedroom. I sat her down on my bed as I headed back toward the kitchen and brought back some of the scented candles that I had brought for this very special occasion.

I lit a few of them as I placed them around the room. I walked over to where she was sitting and began placing feather light kisses on her chocolate skin. I pulled away briefly as I began to undress. Janae watched me under hooded eyes as I dropped my boxers and began to stroke my rock-hard dick. She licked her lips as I walked over to her, pulled off her boots, and began to undress her. I took a step back for a brief moment as I stared at her sexy body before I slid between her legs. I never was the type of nigga to stick it without giving my girl some head. I kissed her from her neck all the way down to her pussy. I slid my tongue in and out of her treasure box as I caressed her clit. Her moans had a nigga ready to fuck, but I held my desires at bay because I wanted to show Janae just how much I wanted and needed her in my life. I was determined to give her the best dick that she had ever had. I licked and sucked on her pussy until her legs began to shake and she screamed out my name like she was at church worshipping on a Sunday morning.

I licked her body up and down just before I slid my tongue into her mouth. I placed my hands on her titties and rubbed her nipples with my fingertips. I pulled away from her as I took each nipple in my mouth and sucked on them until she begged me to give her the dick.

A few moments later, I slid into her, and I swear I felt as if I was home again. Her pussy was tight and juicy just like I liked it. As I stroked her, I gripped her hair gently as I whispered in her ear just how much I loved her. She wrapped her legs around me and began to meet each stroke that I gave her. I pulled away from her briefly as I opened her legs wider and looked into her eyes as I dived in and out of her honey box.

I couldn't even remember the last time that I had even broke Janae off any of this dick. She was supposed to be top priority on my list, but she and I never seemed to have time to just fuck one another. I caressed her titties as I slammed into her a few more times before I pulled out of her and laid on my back so she could ride my dick.

I groaned as Janae straddled me and began to grind that fat pussy on me. I placed my hands on her hips as I rocked her back and forth on my pole as she gently cried out my name.

"Damn, this dick good as hell," she mumbled under her breath as she worked her hips.

I pulled her down toward me and held her as I began to murder her pussy. Her screams in my ear only made me slam into her harder. I slowed down for only a moment as I slapped her ass a few times.

When she told me to fuck her harder, I complied. My headboard banged against my wall as I gave Janae some of this dope dick. When her body began to shake and she screamed out my name, I knew she had already reached her nut and now, it was time for me to reach mine. I held on to her tightly as I slid my finger in her bootyhole. She gasped as I slammed into her a few more times before I shot my nut all up in her.

I was exhausted as hell because I had just busted me a fat ass nut, and all I wanted to do was cuddle up with my girl. Janae had just laid down on my chest, and I was telling her just how much I loved her when her phone began to ring. She groaned when she saw the number on her phone but answered anyway. When she looked back at me, I sat up in bed to see what was up with her.

"I'm sort of preoccupied right now, I can't come in today," Janae spoke softly into the phone.

When she hung up the phone, I was relieved. I blamed her job for the reason that I had been cheating on Janae. She was constantly working, and she rarely got a day off. The times that she would get off, all she wanted to do was sleep, and on my days off, all I wanted to do was fuck. Our schedules were totally different. To be honest, I didn't understand why she felt she had to work in the first place. I had tried talking her into quitting when my company first started booming, but she never would do it.

I looked over at Janae and placed a kiss on her cheek before taking her by her hand and staring into her eyes. I could see into her soul, and I saw love and uncertainty.

"Baby, I know we had this talk a few months back, but I truly think we need to have this talk again."

"What you want to talk about?"

"I honestly think you should quit your job. You went over and beyond to get me that loan to start my own business and even though I paid you back for that shit, I still feel like your ass shouldn't be slaving and waiting tables when you can stay home and look sexy every day. I mean, you ain't getting paid a whole lot of money, and secondly, I make enough at my carwash to take care of you, baby."

Janae stopped me and cleared her throat.

"I understand what you telling me, but I'm not quitting my job. I was always raised to never depend on a nigga. I never have, and I'm not going to start now. I helped you out of the kindness of my heart. Like you said, you paid me back in full, and I'm thankful for that, but that don't mean I expect for you to take care of me."

I sighed with frustration. Janae was stubborn as hell. It was time that I was flat brutal with her ass.

"Janae ask yourself how much free time you actually have? Shid, while I was fucking you, I couldn't even remember the last time you had even given me the pussy.

You constantly working and never have time to even suck a nigga dick."

She was just about to cut me off, but I wasn't having it. I was about to let her ass know the truth.

"You know I'm addicted to the pussy, and you wasn't giving none up."

I was just about to say more when Janae slapped me across the face.

"Nigga, I know you ain't trying to blame me for the reason why you was fucking with that nasty bitch!" she yelled at me.

I looked at her ass like she was crazy.

"If you would have been doing your job, Janae, I wouldn't have to go fuck another bitch."

This conversation wasn't going how I wanted it to go, and Janae was looking at me like she wanted to murder a nigga.

"I'm just being honest with you."

Janae was pissed and hopped off the bed as she tried to search for her clothes. There was no way that I was about to let her leave my place angry, so I pushed her small ass up against the wall. She kicked and screamed, but I pinned her ass down and told her she wasn't going anywhere until she calmed down.

"If you don't want to quit, don't, but stop taking on so many hours to the point where you are drained when you come home, and you can't even give me no sex."

Janae rubbed her hands through her hair before she stared into my eyes and nodded her head. I let her go because she seemed like she had calmed down.

"Baby, I don't want you mad at me, and I don't want to cheat on you either."

Janae nodded her head but didn't speak for the longest moment. When tears began to fall from her eyes, I quickly wiped them away.

"I'm not going to lie. I admit, I've been working longer hours than usual these past six months, but I never thought of you while I was doing any of this. Your feelings never came into my mind when I started working double shifts. Some of it was out of my control though, but I understand what you saying."

I stopped her from her long-winded speech and kissed her on her soft, plump lips.

"I'm just glad you and I talked about this. I don't want to lose you, Janae. I love you."

When we pulled away from one another, I felt that the issue that was ruining our relationship had been solved. I was a firm believer that talking shit out in a relationship always would benefit both parties. Janae now understood how I felt, and I also understood how she felt. I just hoped from now on our relationship could grow and become stronger.

PRINCESS

I felt like a zombie. It had been over a week, and I hadn't heard a word from Cameron. I checked the news every day thinking that somebody was going to report on his story, but nothing ever was said. Every morning, I woke up believing that it was going to be the day that I heard Cameron's sexy voice again. I went to work every night, did my job, brought my ass home, and got in bed. It was a routine for me. I felt like my life was over with. I had never been this depressed in my life. I couldn't wrap my mind around what the fuck was going on with me. I was feeling things about this nigga that a bitch would normally feel about a nigga that she had been fucking around with for at least a year. Cameron and I had only kicked it for two weeks, but during those two weeks, I had become attached to him. I never imagined that he and I would be separated this early in the game.

I looked over at my clock, and it read 9:00 p.m. I had been tossing and turning for over an hour, but I couldn't rest. As I laid there and stared up at the ceiling, I made a promise to myself that the next time I ever talked to Cameron, I was going to tell him exactly how I felt about him. No longer was I going to hold back the intense love that I had for him. I had learned the hard way that you never knew when the person you care about would be taken away from you. I had a deep connection with a man who I hadn't even known for six months, and I wasn't ashamed of it. Everything always happened for a reason, and I was a firm believer in that.

All of a sudden, a calmness washed over my nervous body, and a few moments later, my cell began to ring. It was from a number that I didn't recognize. Normally, I didn't answer numbers that I didn't know, but something in my heart told me that this phone call was going to change my life.

"Hello."

"Princess, are you okay? Did I wake you?"

My heart skipped a beat when I heard Cameron's voice in my ear. I sat up in bed as I tried to gather up my composure to answer his question.

"Princess, are you still there?"

Tears fell down my cheeks because I was just that happy to hear from him.

"I'm here," I choked out.

"Princess, I'm sorry about how shit went down. I would have been called you, but I had a lot of shit I had to figure out. I hope you know that I've thought about you every day. I wish I would have taken you up on your offer to stay at your place. I never thought that the bitch I was loving was really the enemy."

I listened to him as he talked to me about his case and what the Feds were trying to charge him with. He had over three charges, and I feared for the worst. The fact that he had a drug charge was what scared the living shit out of me. They had over six months of evidence on his ass, and he was facing over ten years in prison if he didn't get his charges dropped.

"Princess, I hate that you and I didn't get the chance to explore our feelings before all this happened."

"I know," I groaned.

I wiped the tears that had fell from my eyes as I tried to keep myself calm.

"I just want you to know that no matter what happens, I'm going to keep in touch with you as long as you are willing to answer my calls."

"When will I hear from you again?"

"You will hear from me tomorrow. I promise. Right now, I'm sharing this phone with another guy until I get my own."

"Princess, I know you don't owe me any type of loyalty since you and I haven't known each other long, but—"

I cut him off mid-sentence and told him exactly how I felt about him. It was time that he knew the feelings that were burning in my heart.

"Cameron, I'm willing to do whatever I can to help you out in your time of need. When I met you, I felt something, but I had no clue what it was. I felt this pull with you, but I never understood why. You set my soul on fire. I never felt this way about anyone in my life. I don't know what it is about you, but I'm eager to find out."

"Princess, I feel the same way about you. The first time I saw you crying on that windowsill, I swear my heart broke. I wanted to protect you to make you feel better. After we started spending time with one another, I couldn't stop the feelings that I was feeling. Two weeks ain't long, but I feel like I've known you for two years."

"I feel the same way," I replied truthfully.

Cameron and I talked for over twenty minutes about our feelings for one another before he gave me the number to his lawyer and told me to call him in the morning so he could see if his charges could be dropped.

After the call was disconnected, I lay in bed and stared up at the ceiling. I replayed our phone conversation over in my head until I fell into a deep sleep.

When his lips met mine, I knew that he was the one who was going to make all my hurt and pain go away. He rubbed his hands through my hair as he placed feather light kisses on my neck and chest.

"Baby, I love you," Cameron whispered in my ear just before he unzipped my black and beige spandex dress. As the dress fell to the floor, I felt his hands roaming my body. I moaned softly as he picked me up and placed me on the kitchen counter. He grabbed my hand and placed it on his dick as he stared into my eyes. My pussy tingled as I waited for him to enter me.

When he slid his tongue into my mouth, my knees went weak, and my pussy was dripping wet. He pushed my legs apart as he stepped between them.

He snatched my thong to the side and was just about to enter me... when I woke up to my alarm clock.

I sat up as I pushed the covers from my body and stepped out of bed. I headed straight to the shower to clean myself because my dream had a bitch hot as hell. After I stepped out the shower, I hit up Cameron's lawyer like he told me. I talked to him for over ten minutes before we hung up, and I headed to KFC to do my eight hours. When I pulled up at KFC, I knew some shit must have popped off because the police had the whole place surrounded. I parked in my usual spot as I headed into the building. I was just about head to clock in when I saw three police officers coming from the back with Dee in handcuffs. I stared at her as my mouth dropped open. I never expected to come to work to find her ass being lead out by police officers. She didn't speak to anyone. Instead, she had her head down. Her weave covered her face as she was led to one of the police cars.

"What in the hell just happened?" I asked no one in particular as I watched the last police car pull out the KFC driveway.

"Word was that she was driving drunk and killed someone."

I placed my hands to my mouth. Even though Dee and I had never seemed to get along, my heart still felt an ounce of pity for her. Vehicular Manslaughter and DUI? Lord, she was going to be going away for a long time.

My coworkers were just about to start gossiping until our second in command walked into the restaurant looking like she had been ran over by a train. Her hair was scattered, and her clothes looked wrinkled.

"Hey, everyone. Sorry I'm late. I was called in at the last minute to fill in for Dee," Shay responded.

Everyone acknowledged her before they got back to work.

"If you need me, I will be in the back," Shay said.

The whole time I was at work, it was drama free. I did my job and clocked out. Shay acted totally different than Dee. After I clocked out, I was getting ready to head home when I received a call from the same number that Cameron had called me from the night before.

When I heard his voice, it brightened my day. He asked about my day, and I told him about Dee. We talked for a little while longer before he told me that he was getting ready for his lawyer to meet up with him so they could come up with a game plan. After we hung up the phone, I began to pray that the Lord set him free.

*****

TWO WEEKS LATER

I had just pulled up at my spot and parked beside Darnell's and Janae's cars. I was shocked to see Janae home because normally, she would be at work around this time. I stepped in the house and wished I had kept on driving. I wasn't expecting on walking into a sex fest.

Wine bottles were thrown on the floor while empty beer bottles were strewn all over the living room coffee table. The smell of weed hit my lungs as I walked farther in the apartment.

"Janae!" I called out.

A few moments later, I heard screaming and banging as Janae ran into the living room half ass naked with Darnell running behind her with his shirt off.

"What y'all fools got going on?" I asked them.

Janae tried covering herself, but it was too damn late. I had seen way too much damn skin.

"I didn't know you were going to be off today?" Janae tried to play it off.

I stared at her and pointed at her little Indian outfit.

"The question is... what you doing off?"

Darnell came from behind her and grabbed her on her hips before placing some kisses on her neck. Janae closed her eyes as she basked in his love.

"I will be in the bedroom waiting on you," he told her sexily.

Janae nodded her head as she looked back toward him.

"I know. I normally be at work, but I decided to cut back on some of the long hours."

I smirked at her because it was miracle. This bitch was working hours like she was Superwoman.

"I had to cut back or risk losing my man, and I didn't want to lose him."

"I understand that, boo. I'm glad you and him are trying to work things out."

"Me too. I don't see life without him in it," Janae replied emotionally.

"As long as you're happy, I'm happy," I told her before blowing her a kiss and telling her I was going to head back out to give them some time to themselves.

I had just stepped back in my car when I checked my phone. I was shocked to see that I had just gotten a text message from Cameron telling me that he was thinking about me and he had put me on his list to come see him in the county jail. I held the phone to my chest because tomorrow was Saturday, and I was going to take my ass to the jail to see him if I could.

I quickly texted him back to let him know that I was going to visit him tomorrow, and I couldn't wait to see him again. We texted each other back and forth until he told me that he was going to call me back later on that night.

****

THE VISIT

I was nervous as hell, but as soon as I stepped through the door and saw Cameron sitting at the table waiting for me, I began to calm down. He was rocking an orange jumpsuit that had *Houston County Jail* printed on the back. He stood up and embraced me before we took a seat.

Even though Cameron was locked up and no longer rocking his fancy clothes or shoes, he was still looking sexy as hell. I licked my lips as I stared over at him. He smirked because he must've known exactly what I was thinking.

When he told me I was looking sexy as hell, my heart fluttered by just the tone of his voice. How he was glaring at me he acted like he wanted to strip my clothes off right then and there and fuck the shit out of me. I was dressed in a pair of skinny jeans with the knees ripped, a pair of brown ankle boots, and a thin brown sweater. My Remy hair was bone straight with a small amount of makeup.

"I'm not going to lie, I didn't know for sure if you was even going to show up," Cameron confessed.

"I told you over the phone that I was not going to leave your side."

Cameron sat back in his chair and glared at me as if he was sizing me up to see if I was telling the truth.

"So, are you telling me that you willing to wait ten years for me to come back to you if I had to serve that long ass sentence they trying to throw at me?"

I looked at him for a moment and couldn't stop the emotions that were circling around my heart. I know it sounded crazy as hell, but I was willing to wait as long as I could for Cameron to come home. He was the only man who had my full attention. There was no other nigga who could come into my life and turn me against him at any given time.

I placed my hands on the table before I stared at him with a serious expression on my face.

"Ten years is a long time, Cameron, but I'm willing to wait as long as I can for you to get out. I'm not perfect. and I'm not going to lie and say that I can pull it off for ten years, but I'm willing to give you my heart right here and now. "

I must have said all the right things because he smiled and grabbed my hand from across the table and kissed it.

"I just wished I would have met you earlier. I wouldn't be sitting here."

"I know what you mean," I whined.

"Well, I don't want to scare you, talking about me doing ten years."

I eyed him because he had a smirk on his face.

"My lawyer came by, and we talked. He's going strong as hell on my case. I will be up out this bitch very soon."

"When?" I asked desperately.

"I say the most that I'll have to do is six months. Do you think you can wait six months, Princess?"

I pushed his hands away from me and laughed at his crazy ass.

"Of course, I can wait six months, nigga."

His eyes sparkled as he took me all in.

"Nigga, why you up here telling me this sad story about ten years."

"Because I wanted to see where your mind was at."

I shook my head at him.

"You play too much," I joked.

"Don't panic. You answered correctly, baby."

My heart fluttered. This nigga had never called me "baby." I knew right then that he and I had just gone to the next level in our relationship.

"Before you have to go, I want to ask you something."

"What do you want to ask me?"

"Are you ready to be mine?"

I wasn't expecting him to even ask me that question, especially while he was locked away and wearing an orange jumpsuit.

"If you don't want to answer, that's fine too."

"I'm sorry. I just wasn't expecting you to ask me something like that."

My palms were sweating, and my nerves was shot. I stared into his eyes and felt pulled into his world.

"Yes, I will be yours. I don't want anyone else," I heard myself say.

Cameron nodded his head before he placed one last kiss on my hands and stood up. He embraced me and placed a kiss on my lips just before the door opened behind me. My knees were weak, and I felt like I was about to pass out when his lips left mine. I looked back once as the guard grabbed Cameron and took him back. My heart broke because I was going to be leaving by my damn self, and he wasn't with me. As soon as I got in my car, I dialed Janae's number and prayed that she picked up. I needed to talk to someone, and she was the only bitch I knew that I could trust.

I swerved and weaved through traffic as the rain beat down on my Acura. I threw the phone on the passenger seat when Janae's voicemail came on. This bitch was supposed to be off today, and she wasn't even picking up the phone. I pulled into my place but didn't see her car, so I figured she was probably with Darnell somewhere. When I stepped in the house, I began to get naked and hopped in the shower.

As the water pounded down on my body, all I could think about was Cameron and the conversation that we shared earlier. I couldn't help but smile when he asked me if I could be his girl. It wasn't going to be long before Cameron came home. I just prayed that I was able to handle the love that he and I shared. Six months was going to go by fast, and then he was going to be home again. A lot of niggas said a lot of shit they didn't mean when they were locked the fuck down, so I began to have doubts if he even truly wanted to be with me or if he just wanted me to ride with him until he was released. As soon as that thought crossed my mind, I immediately removed that negative energy from my brain. Cameron was being real with me. There was no way that he was playing games. For the first time, I said a silent prayer for my heart and sanity that all went well.

CAMERON

A nigga couldn't believe it. Here I was sitting in the county jail all because I trusted a bitch. Damn, I never saw it coming, but I should have been smarter than I had been. I always preached to Icey J about trusting bitches, and here I was falling into the trap of a worthless ass bitch. As I laid on my cot, I still couldn't get over the betrayal. If I ever saw that bitch again, I was going to put a bullet in her head. I wanted her ass dead, but there was no way I wanted to be linked to her murder. The bitch had set me up, and I was big on loyalty, which she didn't even have.

My whole vibe changed when I started thinking about Princess. Damn, it was something about Princess that had a nigga's head gone. She had some type of effect on me that I couldn't shake. When she told me that she was willing to try to wait on me for ten years, I knew that she was the one for me. She had come to visit a nigga when she could have forgot about me and went on with her life. She and I had no history together. We only had shared two weeks with one another before the Feds scooped a nigga up.

I promised myself as I looked up at the ceiling that when I got free, I was going to treat Princess like the queen that she truly was. She was going to get one hundred percent of my loyalty. Even though I promised myself that I was never going to trust another bitch, there was something in my heart that told me that Princess was different from the rest of these other hoes. She deserved the best in life, and I was willing to give her the world if she wanted to stand by my side.

After my thoughts left Princess, I started to think about my right-hand nigga, Icey J. His charges were dropped because they really wanted me. He was the first person I called when I got ahold of a phone in this bitch. I told him what the deal was. He stayed in hiding for over three days before my lawyer told me that his charges were dropped because I was the one who they were really investigating. I was relieved because I knew Icey J was going to get shit back running for when I got back home again. I wasn't complaining about how nothing went down because it could have been worse. I could be facing ten years or more, but now I was looking at less than six months, so that was a blessing in itself. Even though I wasn't a religious person, I knew that there was God up there looking down on me. I quickly thanked him for stepping in before sleep found me.

****

A FEW DAYS LATER

I had Icey J pay my lawyer over $10,000 to get my ass out of the ten-year deal, and this nigga had come through for me. I was sitting in a small ass courtroom with a bunch of high powered white people and didn't sweat one time because I knew my attorney had the power to make their asses drop almost every charge. My lawyer, who told me to call him Darren, was a dark-skinned ass nigga rocking a bald head and looked like he was in his forties. He had made a name in the streets as the best attorney to book if you had the bread to afford him. He was tall, muscular, and didn't talk much. When he did say some shit, it was some real shit that was coming out his mouth. He was dressed in an all-black Gucci suit, a pair of black Gucci shoes, and was staring at the prosecutor as they tried to gather up the little evidence they had.

After all sides had been heard, the judge came to an agreement that the prosecution didn't have enough evidence to send my ass hiking. I could see the anger on his face as he turned as red as a tomato. He knew and I knew that he had over six months of evidence on my ass, but even though he had all that shit on me, it wasn't nothing that he could do because my bread and connections were way longer than his.

I smirked when the judge told us that I only had to serve four months in jail, and then I could be released. It was December, so that meant my ass wasn't going to get out until April, but I was good with that shit. Four months was better than ten years.

As soon as I went back to my cell, I was itching to get the phone so I could call Princess. I got the phone a few moments later, and I shot a text to Icey J to let him know that a nigga was coming home in April. He quickly shot a message congratulating me. He also told me that everything was running smoothly on the streets, and he had gotten another trap house that was bringing in even more money than the first one. When he told me he was going to put some money on my books, I thanked him before I hit my baby up. Her phone rang once before her beautiful voice filled my ears.

"Baby!" she yelled into the phone.

My heart sung because hearing her voice really brought joy to my heart. Being locked up wasn't a joke, so I was constantly looking forward to hearing from her ass. The fact that every time I hit her line she was happy to talk to a nigga, let me know she was down for a nigga.

"Baby, where you at?" I asked her.

"I'm driving. I'm about to head to KFC to make this day."

I swear my baby was strong as hell. She dealt with so much shit every day on that damn job, but her ass was committed, and I loved that about her. I wanted nothing more than to tell her sexy ass to tell KFC to kiss her ass, stay her beautiful ass at home, and let me take care of her.

As soon as I got my ass back out on the streets, I was going to see how she felt about me taking care of her. If she still wanted to work, then I understood that too. But if she didn't, then I wanted her to know I had her back.

"Baby, I've missed you!" she yelled into the phone.

I smiled.

"I've missed you too, boo. I got some good news for you, baby."

"Tell me," Princess demanded happily.

I chuckled.

"I'm coming home in April."

Princess screamed into the phone.

"Are you serious?"

"Yes, baby, serious as a heart attack."

"This really made my day. You just gave me the motivation to head into work and get this check."

I laughed at her silly ass.

"Is your shift leader still giving you a hard time?"

"Hell nawl. She got locked up."

"Hold the fuck up? She did?"

"Hell yes, she ran somebody over. My shift leader now is cool as fuck. I'm still working hard as hell, but I ain't got to deal with Dee talking shit to me."

I felt better that Dee wasn't making Princess's life a living hell no more, but I didn't wish prison on nobody.

"Baby, I just want you to know if you need anything, just let me know. You know I got you."

"Thanks, baby, but I got this," she replied.

I figured her pride wasn't going to let her take anything from me. She and I were going to have to talk about that shit.

She and I laughed and talked for a few more moments before she told me that she had just made it to work and she had to go. After our call was disconnected, I went about my day and kept myself busy until I heard my baby's voice again.

****

TWO WEEKS LATER

CHRISTMAS DAY

It was Christmas day, and I was locked up. If I was out on the streets, I would have dropped two racks on my girl if I had one at the time. I was in my own world, waiting for the guards to do count before I pulled out my cell. I heard the footsteps of the guard. When they called my name and told me I was having visitation, my heart dropped. I followed the guard and waited until she locked the door behind me. Princess stood up from where she was sitting and embraced me. Her perfume filled my nose, and with her soft body pressed up against mine, my dick was on hard.

She must have felt my dick print on her because her eyes grew big.

"All this dick is yours when I come home."

She blushed, which had a nigga wanting to bend her over right then and there. I hadn't had any pussy in over a month, and she was looking mighty fine with her Christmas leggings and a plain red spandex sweater that hugged her juicy titties. I rubbed my fingers through her soft hair before placing a kiss on her juicy lips. Her cherry lip gloss covered my lips, but I didn't give a damn.

"Merry Christmas, baby," I whispered in her ear.

She smiled before she told me the same.

"I wasn't expecting you to come by," I admitted.

"Now, you should have known that I wasn't going to leave you here to spend your Christmas alone. You should know me better than that."

"Yes, I should have known you was going to pull up on me."

She and I talked for over two hours before she told me she had to go.

I didn't want her to leave my side, but I hugged her and told her to drive safely.

I told her to keep her phone on her because I was going to hit her up in another hour. When her lips met mine, my dick jumped. I was craving her, and it was killing me that I couldn't have her. After she dipped out, I headed back to my cell and hit Icey J up.

He picked up on the first ring and told me Merry Christmas. He and I talked and joked around for a good ten minutes before I gave him Princess's number and told him to give her two stacks out of my stash for Christmas.

"Damn, nigga, you must really love her ass to give her two stacks and you ain't even fucked her yet."

I laughed because Icey J was correct. I was in love with Princess. She had a nigga sprung, and I hadn't even sampled the pussy yet.

When I told him that she had come to see me, he really went in on my ass.

"Maybe this time you hit the jackpot. If she was willing to wait on your ass with that long ass sentence they was trying to throw at you, then you got you the real deal. Shorty got mad love for you."

Icey J and I talked for a little while longer before I heard his girl in the background fussing about some bullshit he had done. Icey J told me he had to go and told me he was going to give Princess her money also.

After we disconnected the call an hour later, I got a text from Icey J letting me know that he had dropped Princess off her money. It wasn't even twenty minutes later that my phone lit up, and I saw Princess's number on my screen.

I already knew this was going to be a long ass conversation. She told me how much she was thankful for the money and what all she was going to do with it. I listened to the excitement in her voice. I felt good knowing that I had something to do with her happiness. After over two hours of talking, I had to dip because it was dinner time.

PRINCESS

4 months later...

Every night, I went to bed alone and got up the next morning to an empty bed. Every night, for four months straight, I laid in bed wishing that my man was lying beside me. Every morning, I counted down the days until Cameron was going to be released. I didn't know how I got through those four months, but with the grace of the man above and my best friend, Janae, I had survived the cold, lonely nights. I found myself getting off work every day and waiting by the phone for my baby to call or text me. When it got closer to him coming home, Icey J sent me another two stacks and instead of me putting it in my savings account and being responsible, I went and blew a thousand on new clothes, designer shoes, and purses. I got all types of shit that I knew was going to grab his attention and purchased a drawer full of lingerie.

It was Wednesday. I had just pulled up at KFC when I got a text message from Icey J stating that Cameron was getting out the next day. Hearing the good news had a bitch excited as hell. I hopped out my car and was ready to get my shift over so I could take my ass home, take me a long bath, and get some sleep. I didn't want to be tired when my baby came home.

It was 8:00 p.m., and I was halfway through my shift when one of my coworkers called out my name saying they needed some help up front. I headed up front, covered in flour from prepping chicken. I almost fell out when I saw Cameron posted up by the drink machine. He was dressed in a pair of black cargo shorts, a pair of white and red Jordans, and a white and red Jordan shirt. His dreads were pulled back in a ponytail, and the diamonds in his ears and nose gleamed in the light. He was rocking a long silver chain around his neck with a diamond chrome watch on his wrist. Tears fell from my eyes as I screamed and ran toward him. I jumped on him and wrapped my legs around his waist as he held me in a tight embrace. He held me for the longest time as I tried to squeeze the life from his body. When he put me down and his tongue slid into my mouth, I literally felt weak in the knees, and he had to hold my ass until I regained my footing.

"Baby, you out early. Icey J told me that you wasn't going to get out until tomorrow."

"I wanted to surprise you, baby."

"You literally gave me a heart attack. I've missed you so fucking much."

"I've missed you too, lil' mama. I'm all yours now."

I brushed up against him, and his dick quickly began to get hard.

"Don't even play with me because if you do, I don't mind by taking you in that bathroom and bending your ass over."

I was just about to respond when my shift leader, Shay, came out from the back and told me that I could leave. She didn't have to tell a bitch twice. I grabbed Cameron by his hands and pulled his sexy ass out the door. Cameron laughed as we hopped in his car and hit the road.

"What we going to do about my car?"

"Don't worry about all that. Icey J on his way to pick it up and drop it at your place."

I leaned back in the seat with relief.

"Where you want to go first?"

I looked over at this nigga like he was crazy. Instead of responding, I placed my hand on his thigh and began to caress him as he drove.

"If you keep touching on me like that, I might just pull over on the side of the road and give you this dick right now."

I laughed and removed my hand.

A few moments later, we pulled up at my place. I was grateful as hell when I noticed that the apartment was dark and Janae's car was gone. We hopped out, and he beat my ass to the door. We were so horny for one another that we didn't even make it to the bedroom before he and I began to get naked. He kissed on my body as he pulled off my KFC shirt. My body shook with anticipation as he pulled away, unzipped his shorts, and pulled them off. When we were undressed, he placed his lips on mine, and my knees began to shake as I felt my soul was on cloud nine. I felt like I had smoked a fat ass blunt. I didn't hesitate to get on my knees and begin to please him with my mouth. When his hands gripped my hair, I sucked him harder as I rubbed on his balls. I pulled his dick out my mouth and began to suck and lick on his balls as he moaned my name.

When I looked up at him, he was looking right back at me as he continued to push his dick in and out of my wet mouth. I sucked and licked his head before I pulled him out my mouth and sucked him back in as if my mouth were a vacuum. The way he was moaning had my pussy dripping wet. A few moments later, he pulled his dick out of my mouth before he laid me down on my bed and slid his tongue between my thighs. My eyes rolled to the back of my head as his tongue began to please me.

"Shit," I whined as his tongue caressed my clit. My pussy was dripping as he slid a finger into me and continued to suck and lick on my sensitive clit. The way he was sucking on my clit, I didn't want him to stop. When my legs began to shake, I cried out his name over and over until my juices began to flow from my pussy. He licked me clean before he slid two fingers into my entrance and sucked each of my nipples.

"Baby," I managed to choke out.

I wanted to say more, but I couldn't find the words. I was experiencing so much pleasure that I didn't want it to end.

"You just don't know how long I have waited for this day. You just don't know how many nights I thought about sliding in and out of this pussy," he whispered into my ear before he slid his rock-hard dick into my fat pussy. My pussy walls clenched as his dick invaded my walls.

I bit down on my lips and grabbed my titties while he stroked me with his magic stick.

"Is it good, baby?" Cameron asked gently.

"Yes, baby, it's the best I ever had," I replied emotionally.

He chuckled before he slid more of his dick into me and embraced me as he gently pulled on my hair and gave me some gentle, deep strokes.

"Baby, I love you," he groaned into my ear as I wrapped my legs around his waist.

Tears fell from my eyes because we were making passionate love, and he had just told me he loved me.

"I love you too," I choked out as he grabbed my ass cheeks and began to plump faster into my honey box.

He pulled away for a moment before he pulled me on top of him. I looked down at him as he began to play with my titties. I moaned as his dick slid into me. He placed his hands on my hips as I began to slow grind on his dick. He smacked my ass a few times as I began to bounce up and down on his rock-hard pole. I wasn't showing his dick any mercy as I rode him into oblivion. Our tongues danced together as he began to pound inside my tight pussy. I cried out his name as he held me in his arms as he began to fuck me harder.

I screamed when he bit me gently on my neck and smacked my ass.

I yelled out when he placed the tip of his finger in my ass and murdered my pussy. My body began to shake as I began to milk his dick with my cum. Not long after, he shot his hot semen into my pussy.

He and I laid next to one another, but no words were spoken. Sweat dripped from our bodies as we laid there on top of the covers. I turned over to face him, and when I stared into his eyes, I saw nothing but love in them.

"Was this dick everything you dreamed about?"

"It was perfect, baby. My pussy is still tingling."

He chuckled as he slid off the bed and headed toward the kitchen. I heard him rattling some dishes before he came back five minutes later with a bottle of wine and two wine glasses. I stared at him as he poured our wine and headed toward the bathroom. A few minutes later, I heard the bath water running. I walked into my bathroom and wasn't expecting to see that he had ran me a bubble bath.

The bathroom smelled of peaches, and he was waiting on me to hop in. I walked over to where he was standing and placed a kiss on his lips. One kiss turned into him licking and sucking on my neck, which only made my ass want to fuck. He pulled away first before he stepped his fine ass in the bubble bath, and I followed right behind him. He passed me my wine glass, and we took a few sips before placing them down the floor. He held me as I closed my eyes and leaned back on his strong chest. He massaged my titties before he placed gentle kisses on my shoulders and neck.

After we hopped out the tub, I grabbed a black robe out my closet and handed it to him as I wrapped my body up in a lavender robe. I grabbed the empty wine glasses and headed toward the kitchen where I placed them in the sink. Cameron followed me and grabbed a beer out the fridge before sliding his phone in his robe pocket and taking a seat on the living room couch. When he pulled out his baggy of weed, I already knew it was about to go down. I flipped through the channels on TV until I finally came across a Lifetime movie that grabbed my attention. He lit his blunt, took a few puffs, and passed it to me. I stared at the blunt and tried to decide if I wanted to hit it or not.

"Baby, before I let you hit this blunt, I need to know something."

"What you want to know?"

"Have you ever smoked weed before?"

I laughed because I guess he thought I knew nothing about rolling up because of how I was looking at him. That's where he was wrong. This wasn't my first time hitting a blunt. I hit my first blunt in high school, and I fucked around and got high with Janae's crazy ass. I hadn't hit a blunt in months, and it was looking very tempting.

"Yes, baby, I've smoked weed before."

"Ok. I asked because you looked at me all strange when I passed it to you."

I laughed it off as I took a few puffs and blew the smoke out. We passed the blunt a few times before I started to feel an effect. I headed back in the kitchen, poured me another glass of wine, and brought him another beer. I was just about to sit across from him when he pulled my ass down. I took a few sips of my wine before placing it on the coffee table. He passed me the last bit of the blunt, and I took a few more puffs before I blew the smoke in his mouth and slid my tongue in his mouth. He was just about to open the robe when I heard the keys jingle in the door, which let me know that Janae was home.

When the door opened, Janae stepped in and dropped her keys on the stand. She looked at me and then at

Cameron. I could tell by how she was looking that she was speechless.

"Am I interrupting something?" Janae asked.

"No, girl, you good," I told her calmly as I looked back at Cameron who was putting the last bit of the blunt out.

Janae smirked as she crossed her arms and slammed the door behind her. She looked over at me as she waited for me to tell her exactly who I was smoking and chilling with.

"Janae, this is Cameron. Cameron, this is Janae. She's my best friend and roommate."

Cameron nodded his head and told her that he was glad to meet her. Janae beamed before she walked over to where I stood and grabbed me by my arm.

"Baby, I will be right back," I told Cameron before Janae pulled me into the kitchen.

"Bitch, you better tell me what that sexy ass nigga doing in our damn living room with a damn robe on."

I laughed so hard at Janae's facial expression because I had never seen her ass act that way.

"Is that the same Cameron that had your ass half-crazy and you was crying over?"

I nodded my head to let her know that he was.

"Damn, Princess, you showing out. He look totally different from the men you used to bring up in here." I rolled my eyes at her little slick comment. "I'm so happy for you, sis. I know you glad that he came home."

"Yes, you have no idea. All my lonely nights are finally gone."

"That's good, boo. Well, I'm heading in my room. Darnell coming over later tonight. I got to take a bath and take off these work clothes," Janae replied as she stepped out the kitchen and headed back to the living room to grab her purse.

"It was nice to meet you," Janae told Cameron just before she bent down, picked up her black bag, and headed toward her room to change her clothes and hop in the tub.

When I heard her bedroom close, I looked back at Cameron who was staring daggers at me. He licked his lips at me, and I knew exactly what he wanted. I walked over to where he was now standing at and placed a kiss on his lips. He kissed me back while he caressed my ass. I pulled open his robe and was just about to get down on my knees when he stopped me.

"What about your friend?"

"She in her room taking a bath. Her boyfriend coming over later. It's going to be a while before we hear from her again."

I pulled open his robe, got down on my knees, and took him into my mouth. His moans were really fucking my mind up. I slid his dick in and out my mouth as I caressed my tongue over the tip of his head. I played and squeezed on his balls gently as I slurped on his dick. He pulled my hair with his hand as I began to deep throat his dick. Tears fell from eyes as I felt his dick in my throat. I pulled away briefly only for him to slam his dick back into my mouth until he moaned out my name one last time before he told he was about to nut.

He pulled his dick out my mouth as he nutted on my titties. After he was done I stood up and went to wash myself clean in the kitchen. I was just about to wrap my body back up in my purple robe and head back to my room when Cameron came up from behind me and pressed his hard dick against my ass. He was just about to slide his dick up in my pussy when his phone began to go off. He sighed with frustration and pulled away from me.

I looked over his shoulder and noticed that he was texting Icey J.

"Baby," I mumbled but he didn't answer me.

I closed my robe back and began to pout.

"Baby, I have to go take care of some business."

Tears began to well up in my eyes because I didn't want him to leave my side. He had just gotten out of jail and he was already back out on the streets.

"How long you going to be gone?"

I guess he understood the urgency of him coming back because he told me he would be back before I went to sleep.

I walked him back to my bedroom where I watched him get dressed. I followed him to the door and watched him as he hopped into his car and dipped out.

I closed the door behind myself and pulled out my cell and sent him a quick message to be safe. Never had I ever been a controlling ass female, but when Cameron told me he was dipping out for a minute I wanted to tell him so badly to stay. But I decided to keep my mouth shut, and instead of telling him what to do, I prayed that he came back asap and didn't get in any trouble. There was no way that I was going to be able to go another day without being with him or talking to him. There was no way I wanted to be going visiting my baby in prison ever again.

CAMERON

Damn, a nigga had finally gotten out of jail, and I already was making major moves on the streets. I hated to leave Princess tonight, but I had no other choice. I had shit that needed to be done. As I zoomed and weaved in and out of traffic I couldn't shake Princess from my mind. I couldn't get the image of her sad face out of my head when I first told her I had to leave. As I got closer to my destination, a sense of urgency began to run throughout my veins. All I wanted to do was go in, handle my damn business, and get the fuck out of there. I needed to hurry my ass back to Princess before she ended up regretting giving me her heart.

I wanted to leave the street life alone and cater to my girl, but first before I did any of that, I had to first handle Brianna. I pulled up beside Icey J's custom made Camaro and hopped out. I walked into the warehouse that Icey and I would sometimes use back in the day to push drugs.

I stepped through the double doors, and that's when I noticed Icey J posted up in the middle of the floor standing in front of a blindfolded and bound Brianna. Her tears and screams began to become louder when she heard Icey J call out my name. I walked over to her, pulled off her blindfold, and stared into her eyes.

"Please don't do this to me," she cried and pleaded.

I laughed in her face before I grabbed the blunt from Icey J's hand, took a few puffs, and blew it in her face. I smirked when she started to cough. I passed the blunt back to Icey J just before I pulled my machete knife off the table and walked over to where she was sitting tied up in a chair, her wrist and legs were bound by rope.

"I'm going to let you handle your business. I will be in the other room if you need me," Icey commented before he placed his blunt back in his mouth and dipped out.

I wrapped my body in plastic so I wouldn't get any of her blood on any of my clothes. After I was satisfied with putting the plastic over my clothes, I began to pace back and forth. I pointed my knife at her before I began to speak.

"Brianna, you brought this shit on your damn self. You came into my damn life acting like you was down for a nigga, but the whole time your ass was scheming and plotting against me. You know loyalty means everything to me in this business, and you broke my trust. I don't care how hard you cry and what you say, today going to be the last day that your lying ass will ever walk this Earth."

"You will not get away with killing me. Are you dumb? If I go missing the Feds and police are going to come after you."

I looked over at her and squinted my eyes.

"Bitch, don't play with me. We all know that the police isn't going to give two fucks that your ass dead. You already served their purpose. They not going to come looking for me because they don't have enough evidence to accuse me of shit. Bitch, you tried to get me sent to prison for over ten years. I have no mercy for your ass," I told her angrily.

"Please, don't do this."

"Lights out, bitch," I said hatefully.

I was so sick of hearing her talk that I didn't hesitate to slice her throat wide open.

Blood splattered everywhere. I was thankful that I remembered to wrap myself in plastic. I placed the bloody machete back on the table before I called Icey J back into the room to help me get rid of her body. Icey J and I worked for two hours straight with trying to clean up all the evidence so nothing would point to us. After we had disposed of her body, I dapped Icey J up and thanked him for helping me take care of Brianna.

"You know I got you, nigga."

After we had cleaned up the warehouse, Icey J locked the warehouse up and we both dipped out.

I looked down at my phone and noticed it was three in the morning. I was just about to head back to my old spot because I figured Princess had went to sleep on it. It was late as hell, and there was no way I was going to be able to head back over to her spot. When I saw Princess's name pop up on my phone I knew she must have waited up on me.

I answered, and when I heard her voice I felt at peace. All the anger and rage I felt before evaporated from my body.

"Baby, where you at?"

"I'm on the way back to your place. That's if you still want me to come back."

"Of course I want you to come back over here."

"Okay, give me ten minutes and I will be pulling up."

"Okay boo."

Ten minutes later, I was pulling up at Princess's place. I stepped out the car and was just about knock on the door when it opened. Princess was looking sexy as hell with a pair of black booty shorts with a pink tank top. I could see her nipples as they pressed against her tight pink top. She pulled me inside and didn't hesitate to place her lips on mine.

I picked her up with one hand and carried her into her bedroom. I pressed her up against the wall as I began to feel on her ass.

She closed her eyes as she began to moan in my ear.

"Promise me that you will never hurt me," Princess said before staring into my eyes.

"Baby, I promise you that I will never break your heart. You can trust me. Your heart is safe with me," I told her passionately as I placed a kiss on her neck.

****

ONE MONTH LATER

I had been on the streets for only a month, but I had my trap house back popping. I was selling more dope than I was before I had gotten locked up. As usual, I had Icey J as my right-hand nigga. Every day I woke up at eight in the morning and got my day started. I hustled all day, but I always made sure to have my ass home by eleven because I didn't want Princess to feel that I was neglecting her. Shid, a nigga was doing good for himself.

I had my cash flow looking good, and I had a nice girl who truly cared about me. My feelings for Princess grew stronger each day. I loved her ass so damn much and would do anything in my power to keep a smile on her face.

Since I had Princess by my side, a nigga thought about shit differently. I wanted us to have the best in life. I wanted her to have the finer things in life because my baby deserved that shit. I had been out cruising the streets almost all day when I noticed some nice ass houses on the side of the road. They had a sign outside by the road that said they were now leasing. I whipped my car around and pulled into the complex and drove around the neighborhood. I was impressed. Normally I was the type of nigga who was down to rent a one-bedroom apartment or condo, but since I had Princess in my life I wanted something more stable.

The houses were all brick and was big as hell, and they all had a drive-in garage where you could park your car. I didn't hesitate to pull up at the leasing office to see just how much it would cost to rent one of the houses. The door chimed behind me to the let the white lady know up front that I had just stepped inside. I talked to her a few moments about the houses and she quickly handed me a brochure as she gave me the prices that they would cost.

I didn't even flinch when she told me that the rent for a three-bedroom and two bathroom was going to be two thousand a month. The older lady looked up at me as if she was shocked that I was even still there trying to find out more information. I guess she thought that I didn't have any money because I looked like a street nigga. I was dressed in a pair of red Gucci shorts, some black Air Forces, and a black and red Gucci shirt. My hair was hanging down my back and was freshly twisted. I was rocking a pair of diamond chrome earrings in my ear, a diamond stud in my nose, and a silver chromed watch.

When she asked me how early I wanted to move in because she had three homes that was available to move in that day, and she had two more coming available very soon.

"I will get back with you. I got to talk to my girl about it first."

She smiled, shook my hand, and gave me her business card.

****

I held open Princess's door as we headed inside Ruby Tuesday. It was Friday night and Princess was off work, so I decided to take her sexy ass out to eat. We took a seat at a booth and waited for the waitress to bring us a menu so we could see what we wanted to order. A few seconds later, our waitress came and gave us two menus and told us she was going to be back in a few minutes to take our orders.

It didn't take Princess and me long to decide what we wanted to eat. As we waited for the young waitress to come back, Princess and I made small talk. I had been thinking all week about what I was going to do about me and Princess's relationship. I knew I was in love with her and I knew she felt the same. I had been trying to figure out the best time to ask her how she felt about moving into a house with me. I had been turning the question around in my mind all week long because I understood she had her roommate who she was living with. I knew her and Janae was very close, and I didn't want to make it seem that I had swooped in and was taking Princess away. I also didn't want to cause any problems just in case Janae relied on Princess to pay her portion of the rent.

Just when I was about to get up the courage to tell Princess about the new house that I wanted us to get, our waitress came back. I looked her over and guessed that she was about eighteen. She looked very young in the face and was rocking some silver braces in her mouth. She was tall, slim, and was the complexion of a dark chocolate candy bar. She looked like she was tired as hell. I could see bags under her eyes and a sense of sadness fell over my soul. She looked like she was overworked and I truly felt sorry for her.

After she had taken our food and drink orders we didn't have to wait long to eat. As we ate our dinner, Princess talked about her job and how she wished she could quit so she could go back to college and finish working on her Accounting Degree. I knew at this time that talking to Princess about the house and our future was the perfect time.

I sat down my fork, grabbed Princess's hand, and stared into her eyes.

"Baby, I have something that I need to discuss with you."

Princess gave me her full attention, and I was grateful. I licked my lips as I told her exactly what was on my mind.

"Baby, I just want you to know that when you came into my life you changed it for me in such an amazing way. I want the best for you, and I don't want you to ever feel that I'm not here for you."

Princess nodded her head as she waited for me to get to the point.

"Baby, if going back to school is what you want to do, then do that shit."

She was just about to cut me off, but I put my hand up to tell her I had more to say.

"Baby, I've fallen deeply in love with you. I want you happy. You have so much more potential than frying chicken all damn day. I got the money to back your ass up with whatever you want to do. I want you to get back in school and make something of yourself."

Tears were falling from Princess's eyes, and I gladly wiped them away.

This was going just the way I wanted it to go. I cleared my throat to let her know that I wasn't finished yet.

"Princess, I've had this on my mind all week long, but I had no clue how I was going to address it to you."

"What else you got to tell me?"

I smiled weakly before I handed her the brochure for the housing Complex called Woodcrest.

Princess opened the brochure and her eyes grew wide when she saw just how beautiful it looked. When she flipped it on the back and noticed the price, she gave it back to me.

"That rent is high as fuck."

I laughed at her expression.

"Baby, do you like it?"

Princess tried to talk, but I hushed her.

"I asked you a question, all I want to hear is a yes or no."

Princess sighed before replying, "Yes."

I smirked.

"Well it's yours. I will seal the deal Monday with Vanessa."

"Who is Vanessa?" Princess asked.

"She is the one who told me to hit her back if I wanted one of these houses."

"Cameron, it's way out of our Price range."

I began coughing because Princess must didn't know how much I was making selling dope.

I raised my eyebrow at her, and she quickly became quiet.

"Princess, I wouldn't have even gave you this brochure if I didn't think I could afford it."

"If you want it, baby, then I will get it for you. I was out riding earlier this week, and I just happened to pass by them and I fell in love with them."

Princess's eyes sparkled.

"I love it. If you can afford it, then you already know what my answer going to be."

I stood up and grabbed her in a hug before placing a kiss on her soft lips.

I pulled away from her first and asked her the question that had been bugging me all week.

"What about Janae?"

Princess placed her arms around my neck before standing on her tiptoes.

"Don't worry about Janae. I will talk to her and let her know what the deal is."

I smacked her ass one good time and left a one-hundred-dollar tip for our young waitress and walked up front to pay the bill. After the bill was paid, I grabbed Princess by her waist and walked her out to the door toward my car. I placed my hand on her thighs as I weaved throughout the Warner Robins traffic. She gently moved my hands and shocked the shit out of me when she unzipped my pants, pulled out my dick, and began to give me some sloppy head. I swear I almost ran into the car in front of me when she started slurping on my dick while she stroked me with her hand.

"Shit," I moaned as I pushed her head further down on my dick until I heard her gag.

She stayed in the position and came up for air a few moments later. I was glad when I pulled my car up at her spot. I cut the car off and leaned my seat back as I enjoyed her giving me some sloppy head. I closed my eyes as I pushed my dick in and out of her mouth as I pulled on her hair.

"I'm about to cum," I choked out.

Princess didn't dare move. Instead, she massaged my balls as she kept her mouth placed firmly on my dick. A few minutes later, I was shooting my hot semen down her throat.

She didn't stop sucking on my dick until she had licked me clean. A few seconds later Janae pulled up right beside my car. Princess and I straightened our clothes up on our bodies before we stepped out the car. Janae had a case load of beer and a big ass brown bag with all types of wine that she had purchased. I was just about to help her bring some of the liquor in the house when her nigga Darnell pulled up. Instead of helping her, Princes pulled me into the house.

"Don't y'all dare go lock up in the bedroom. We about to get fucked up tonight!" Janae yelled out.

JANAE

I had just gotten paid, and a bitch was ready to get drunk and high all night long. When Darnell pulled up behind me, he walked over, smacked me on my ass, and helped me take the all the liquor that I had brought.

"Damn, you brought the whole store," Darnell joked.

"I hope you don't get too drunk, because I don't want to spend my Friday night cleaning up vomit."

"Nigga, don't start that shit. I got this."

"Um, we going to see," Darnell replied.

Time we stepped in my apartment building, I heard Migos "T-Shirt" blasting from my apartment. I grabbed Princess, who was grinding her ass on Cameron, and pulled her into the kitchen so she could help me fix the drinks. We laughed together as we talked about our niggas. We wasn't even gone a minute before we smelled weed.

"Oh shit, you know it's about to go down."

Princess laughed because she already knew I always acted a fool when I got high and got drunk. I switched my sexy ass into the living room and passed the niggas their beers while Princess and I started on our first bottle of wine. I sipped on my drink before I hopped my happy ass back up and started to bounce my ass on Darnell when Gucci Mane started rapping. I was all the way turnt up. Princess passed me the blunt and I took a few puffs before I passed it to Darnell. I danced until my ass got sore and started feeling dizzy as hell. Princess and I had just went through our first bottle of wine and we was drinking on some Hennessy. I was so turnt up that I was drinking the shit straight.

Darnell smacked my ass a few times and as he watched me swing my hips from side to side. I was feeling so good that I didn't even react when the Hennessy started burning my throat. I looked over my shoulder, and that's when I noticed Princess was sitting on Cameron's lap while she smoked on her blunt. I looked back toward Darnell and noticed that this nigga's eyes weres bloodshot red, and he had just lit him another blunt.

Damn, we all was fucked up I thought to myself. I walked my drunk ass over to my phone and switched the music to Chris Brown. I wanted something that would get everyone in the mood to fuck. When I flipped on Chris Brown "To My Bed", I swear that song had me wanting to fuck. I pulled the blunt out of Darnell's mouth and placed a kiss on his lips. I was grinding all on top of him but quickly made a run for the bathroom when I felt the vomit trying to push up my esophagus. I didn't even have time to slam the door shut before I began to empty my stomach. Tears fell from my eyes as I fell to the floor and tried to regain my composure.

"Baby, you okay?" Darnell asked as he walked over to where I was sitting on the floor laid over the toilet seat.

I wasn't trusting myself to get up at the moment; I still felt like I had some more to let out.

"No, baby, I feel awful."

"Baby, you want me to head to Walmart to see if I can find you something to settle your stomach."

I groaned as my head began to ache.

I tried to speak but my words were slurred and my speech was slow.

"Noooo, baby, don't go," I cried out.

"Don't worry, boo. Give me twenty minutes and I will back."

"Do you need for me to carry you in the room?"

I shook my head and mumbled that I was going to stay in the bathroom.

He kissed me on my cheek and promised that he was going to be back soon.

Damn, now I hated I had even fucked around and gotten wasted like I had. I was so gone that I could barely even move. I didn't know exactly where Princess was, but I didn't hear any music blasting from the living room. Everything was quiet until I heard the TV flip on, and then a few moments later I heard the sports channel. Just when I thought it was going to be okay to get up I started right back throwing up. After I had emptied my stomach for the second time I flushed the toilet, pulled myself up off the floor, and wobbled into the living room hoping that Princess was somewhere nearby.

When I stepped in the living room I found Princess laying on the couch fast asleep. The bitch was knocked out with her mouth open, and she was snoring loud as hell. I jumped when I heard Cameron's voice.

"If you coming in here to get Princess, she is knocked the fuck out. She probably ain't going to wake up until in the morning. And when she do wake up, best believe she going to have a hangover."

I groaned as I turned around to face him. When I looked up at him he was holding him a bottle of water and was staring at me with a smirk on his face.

I squinted my eyes as I tried to walk past him, but I accidently lost my footing and fell down.

“Janae, I really think you need to try to sit down somewhere. You drunk as hell. You can barely walk.”

“I’m fine. I’m just waiting on Darnell to hurry back with some medicine.”

“Yeah, I seen him when he dipped out. He said he was going to be back in a bit.”

I nodded my head as reached up and grabbed his outstretched hand. He helped pull me up, and I was grateful. His scent of is cologne tickled my nose as I looked into his soft brown eyes. My heart began to flutter and my stomach felt queasy as I took him all in. Cameron was sexy as hell. He was rocking a pair of white shorts, an all-black shirt, black and white Jordans with a black and white cap that he had flipped to the side. His dreads were pulled back from his face and he was smelling good as hell.

I instantly began to feel guilty as hell because Cameron was Princess’s man. Now I understood why Princess was acting like she was when Cameron had gotten locked up. Cameron had a bitch throbbing between her thighs. I didn’t know why I was lusting after my girl’s man. Maybe it was the alcohol and the weed that I had smoked.

“Where you going?” Cameron asked with worry in his voice when I pulled away from him and tried walking away.

“I’m heading to my room.”

“You ain’t got to act like that. I won’t bite. Princess sleep, and you got Darnell out looking for some medicine. You can sit here and chill with me. Plus, I hate for you to go back there and die of alcohol poisoning.”

I gave him a weird ass look, and he raised his hand at me to let me know that he was only trying to help.

“You have drunk way too much. It’s best you stay with me so I can keep an eye on you.”

I was way too damn drunk to argue with him. Instead I did exactly what he told me. I decided to chill out with him until Darnell came back, which was going to be in any minute. I didn’t dare trust myself to sit anywhere near him. Instead, I headed toward the kitchen, grabbed a chair, pull it into my living room, and took a seat.

Cameron didn’t say anything to me, only shook his head at me as he began to flip through the channels on the TV. My eyes began to get heavy, and I really wanted to fall asleep, but I had no place to lay my head. I looked back at Cameron who was playing with is phone. I looked back over at Princess and noticed she was still knocked the fuck out. Not once had she even moved. I groaned as I stretched and pulled out my phone from my skinny jeans so I could check the time. It had been over an hour and Darnell still haven't gotten back home.

Even though I was drunk, I quickly went into panic mode and decided to call his phone just to make sure he was okay. I called him over five times, and he didn't answer not one call. I left over three voicemails but still didn't get no response from him. After me calling him didn't work, I decided to text him instead. I sent him over ten messages but got no response. By this time, I was trying to sober up somewhat, but I was still out of it. I hopped off the chair and headed toward the kitchen where I grabbed my keys and slid on my house shoes that were located in my bedroom.

I had only one thing on my mind, and that was heading to Walmart to see what the fuck was taking Darnell so long to come back. My mind was going a mile a minute, and I had totally forgotten that Cameron was still present. When he snatched the keys out my hand and grabbed me by my arm I quickly went to reflex mode and hit his ass straight in the jaw.

"What the fuck. Why the hell you just hit me?"

"Look, I don't even know you like that. I don't know why you feel like you can just walk up in here and tell me what to do."

"Look, I'm not trying to tell your ass what to do. I'm just trying to help your ass out."

"Look, I don't need your damn help. Now let me go handle this business. This nigga been gone almost an hour and a half; it don't take that long to bring his ass back".

I was just about to dip out when his ass pushed me up against the wall. I tried pushing him off of me, but I was just way too drunk.

"You ain't about to leave and go nowhere. If you kill yourself, I don't want to hear Princess mouth, and I damn sure don't want it on my conscience."

Cameron was so close to me that if I moved the wrong way his lips would meet mine. I fucked up when I looked into his eyes. It was something about his eyes that had me wanting to lean over and feel his lips on mine. He was smelling so fucking good and he was looking sexy as hell. I had never been this close to Cameron, so I didn't know he was going to have this type of effect on my hormones. I blamed it all on my drinking and figured when I woke up the next morning all the lust that I was feeling for my best friend's man was going to evaporate.

“Will you let me go?” I heard myself beg.

“I will if you promise me you ain’t going to make a run for it.”

“Cameron, look at me. Do it look like I can even run right about now?”

Cameron looked me up and down and smirked.

“I guess you right.”

I was relieved when he released me. Instead of fussing with him I took my ass back over to where I was sitting and took a seat. I pulled out my phone for the last time and dialed Darnell’s number.

Tears began to fall from my eyes because I knew in my heart something wasn’t right. Darnell had never ignored my calls before and always kept his phone on him. Something was going on, and it pained me that I couldn’t do nothing about it.

DARNELL

I looked down at my phone but didn't dare pick it up. I knew that Janae was looking for me and was going to want to know where I was at, but there was no way I was going to fuck around and let her know that I had never even went to Walmart. Tonight was supposed to have been the night that Janae and all us of was going to drink and party, but all that shit came to an end when Lexi texted my phone. At first I ignored her ass, but when she told me that it was very important, I decided to find out exactly what she wanted.

Janae had been throwing up, so I decided to use that as an excuse to dip out for a few minutes to see what Lexi wanted. I told Janae that I was going to head to Walmart to get her some medicine, and I told Princess's boyfriend Cameron to look after her until I got back. Instead of me going to Walmart and trying to find something for Janae to settle her stomach, I went to Lexi's. Soon as I pulled up at her spot, my heart began to speed up because I had a bad feeling that whatever she had to tell me was going to change my life forever.

I knocked on her door only once before Lexi stepped aside to let me in. She was dressed in a pair of hot pink booty shorts with a white tank top. She had her hair pulled back in a ponytail, and her face was freshly scrubbed of makeup. When the door closed behind me, she walked over to me and I could clearly see that she had been crying.

I began to feel uncomfortable because never had Lexi ever cried in front of me. She'd always been the type of bitch to have control over her emotions, and I always respected her for that shit.

"Darnell, I called you over here because I needed to talk to you about something."

I took a seat on the couch as I waited for her to tell me what was so bad that she was crying.

"Darnell, I'm pregnant."

At first I didn't say shit, because I had to make sure I heard the bitch correctly.

"Baby, you ain't going to say nothing?" Lexi cried.

"Hold the fuck up. You pregnant?" I asked her.

"Yes, I'm pregnant."

I sat there and stared at her ass for the longest moment. As I looked more closely at her stomach, I noticed that she did look bloated. Lexi used to have a flat stomach, but now it wasn't so flat anymore.

"Why you looking at me like that?"

"I'm trying to see why you coming at me and telling me that you pregnant, what am I supposed to do about it?"

I already knew what she was getting at. She was basically telling me that I was the father of her baby, and that shit wasn't about to go down.

"I'm telling you because this your child."

I shook my head and stood up. My feelings were all over the place because deep down inside, I knew that I had fucked up.

"Lexi do me a favor and get rid of it. If money is the issue, I will give you some money tomorrow to make an appointment so you can terminate it. I don't want any kids, especially not with you. I'm really trying to do right by my girl, and here you telling me that I got you pregnant."

Tears began to fall from Lexi's eyes as she began to verbally attack me.

"You son of bitch. I'm not killing my baby. This your child, how can you tell me to kill it? You such a heartless ass nigga. Do you think I give a fuck about you in a relationship with Janae? I don't care! If she don't know that you got a child, she soon going to find out!" she screamed.

That was all it took before I pushed her ass up on the wall and began to choke her ass out.

"Bitch, what you ain't going to do is tell Janae shit. You better get that shit out your head if you think I'm going to let you tell her I got you pregnant. Do like I told you and get rid of that baby, before I get rid of you myself," I spat at her.

I released her and she fell to the floor gasping for air.

"Do me favor, lose my number, and stay away from me. You and I are over with, so don't even think you going to use this baby to stay in my life. What you and I had is dead. I don't want you."

I slammed her front door behind me as I dipped out. I was pissed as hell that I had even fucked around and gotten myself in this position. I looked down at my phone and noticed that Janae had just called me. There was no way that I was able to go back to her at this moment. I had to get my mind right. I had to figure out what my next move was because Lexi had just fucked my head all the way up. I had never killed nobody in my entire life but, I was willing to take her ass out if she even thought about ruining what I had worked so hard to rebuild with Janae. I was not about to lose Janae to this bullshit. I knew if Janae found out that I had a baby by Lexi, our relationship was going to be over. I didn't want that to happen.

****

A WEEK LATER

A week had passed by, and my thoughts were all over the place. I did everything in my power to show Janae how much I loved her and needed her in my life. I was thankful that Lexi had left me alone and wasn't trying to cause me any problems. When I opened my eyes, I was grateful to see Janae lying next to me. She opened her eyes a few moments later and placed a kiss on my lips. I pulled the covers away from her half-naked body as I began to kiss and suck on her neck. I trailed kisses all the way down to her stomach just before I moved her gray thong to the side and began to lick and suck on her clit.

She moaned out my name over and over as she pushed my head further down between her legs. I slid a finger into her pussy as I sucked on her clit until her body began to shake and she covered my mouth with her white cream. I licked her clean and was just about to give her some morning dick when my phone began to ring. My heart dropped when I saw Lexi's number pop up on my screen.

"Who calling you this early?" Janae asked.

"Work. Let me take this call baby. I got to make sure the car wash is straight."

Janae pouted, but I kissed her lips and stepped out the room.

I was beyond irritated because I thought I had gotten rid of Lexi, but apparently I hadn't. After I had closed the front door behind me, I hit Lexi back up.

"Did you take care of it?" I asked her.

"What the fuck you mean did I take care of it? You making it seem that our baby is a fucking disease."

I sighed with frustration because I swear I was ready to choke her ass out.

"Look, Lexi, I don't have time for your games. Did you abort the baby like I asked you to?"

"No, I didn't fucking abort the baby."

"I told you I wasn't."

I closed my eyes and said a silent prayer to the man above to give me the strength to get me through this fucked-up situation.

"Lexi, to be honest, I don't give a fuck what you do. You can keep the baby if you want to. But I told you to abort the baby only because I know you thinking in your head if you keep this baby that I will still fuck with you. I'm telling you that I'm not. Why bring a child into this world in this type of situation?"

I was about to say more, but Lexi cut me out.

"Nigga, I don't give a fuck what you say. I'm not aborting my damn child. And whether you want to be with me or not isn't the issue either. I'm having this baby, and you going to take care of it. End of discussion."

I was just about to tell the bitch off, but she had disconnected my call.

I tried calling her back, but she didn't pick up and sent my calls to voicemail.

"Bitch," I mumbled to myself before I headed back into the house.

****

A FEW DAYS LATER

When Janae told me that Princess was thinking about moving out with Cameron she asked me if I wanted to move in with her. Of course I told her I would. Whenever I wasn't at work I was chilling out with Janae, so I didn't see anything wrong about taking our relationship to the next step and moving in with her. When Janae cut down on her hours at work, I swear I saw a difference in our relationship. We were vibing so good, and we were getting along so well with one another. Never did I ever think my world was going to come crashing down.

I had just stepped out the shower when Janae busted open the door screaming and yelling at me. At first I didn't know what the fuck she was talking about until she threw me my half dead phone. I knew instantly that she knew about Lexi and the secret that I was hiding.

"How could you? When was you going to tell me about you getting that bitch pregnant?"

I tried to speak, but Janae attacked me instead. I tried holding her ass down, but she fought me like I was a man. I pushed her on the bed, which only pissed her off more. When she ran toward the kitchen, I already knew what was up. I was fully dressed by the time she came back with a butcher knife.

She pointed her weapon at me. I could see the anger in her eyes, and I understood her pain. There was no way I was about to nut up on her because she was acting crazy. I understood why she was flipping out. If I was her, I would have been flipping out also.

"I loved you. I gave you my all. I took your ass back and this how you repay me? You not only cheat on me, but you got the bitch pregnant. You didn't even tell me. I had to go through your phone and find the shit out."

"Baby, I'm so sorry. I'm going to handle it, I promise. I ain't fucked with Lexi in over three months."

Janae laughed evilly.

"I don't give a fuck if you fucked her yesterday. You got the bitch pregnant. You was fucking the bitch raw and shit. My heart barely got over you cheating on me with the bitch for six months, now I find out the bitch is pregnant with your child. I will never forgive you for that shit."

Hearing her say some shit like that really brought tears to my eyes. My heart felt as if it had been ran over by a train and sliced into tiny small pieces. No, this couldn't be it. This couldn't be the end of our relationship. Just when I had put it in my mind to do right, now I was on the verge of losing her forever.

"Baby, please. When I tell you I'm going to handle this, I'm telling the truth.'

Her hands shook as she held the knife tightly in her grip.

"How you going to make this right? It's nothing that can be done, Darnell. You have went way too far. Cheating on me was fucked up for you to do, but to bring a seed into this world then, that's something I can't overlook."

Tears were falling from her eyes, and my heart broke in half.

"Just get the fuck out my face right about now."

I tried speaking, but she dropped the knife on the floor and walked away from me. I grabbed her, but she quickly snatched her arm away from me.

"Don't touch me. Now do me a favor and get the fuck out my face because if you don't, I promise you how I feel right about now, I will put your ass six feet deep. Right now I don't give a fuck about going to prison."

I let her go and decided the best thing to do was get the fuck out of there and wait until she cooled off.

*****

A FEW HOURS LATER

I had just pulled up at my spot when I noticed Lexi was posted up at her car. I wasn't in the damn mood right about now, and here she was popping up at my spot like I had invited her ass. She was dressed in a pair of white shorts, black flip flops, with a black top. She was rocking a pair of Gucci shades and her hair was flat ironed boned straight and stopped at her ass. She was looking thick as hell. If I wasn't so pissed at her for ruining my life I would have loved to get between her thighs. When I hopped out the car, she walked over to where I was and began to talk her shit.

"I've been calling your ass all week long. I don't like the fact that you was calling me every day to fuck, but now that I'm carrying your seed, you want to ignore my ass."

I closed my eyes and counted to ten before I fucked around and knocked this bitch out.

"Lexi, why the fuck are you over here? I didn't call your ass to come by, so why the fuck you popping up at my spot?"

"Because your ass been avoiding me, nigga. How else am I supposed to be get in touch with you?"

When I looked down at her, I really regretted ever fucking around with her. She had ruined everything for me.

"I don't got shit to say to your ass. I already told your ass how I feel about the shit. If you want to keep the baby then do what you got to do, but don't think that I'm going to be with you or continue to help your ass out."

I was just about to walk into my spot when this bitch had nerve to punch me in the back of my head.

I didn't even think or hesitate before I punched her ass slam out. Tears fell from her eyes as she laid on the ground rubbing her cheek.

I bent down to help her up and to tell her I was sorry, but the bitch snatched away from me and told me to not touch her. I watched as she hopped in her car and pulled off in a hurry. I looked down at my hands and noticed her blood covering my knuckles. I never was the type of nigga to hit a female, but she had really tried my ass up and I had lost my temper for a quick minute. I just prayed after she took that lick that shit didn't get worse for me.

****

<u>A FEW DAYS LATER</u>

I hadn't been to my car wash Bustin' Bubbles in over a week. I could barely get out of bed, and I could barely eat. My heart was broken, and the fact that Janae wasn't picking up her phone and wouldn't text me back when I would text her really hurt me to my heart. I had rode past her spot almost every day, but I never had the courage to stop and knock on the door. I knew if she knew it was me knocking she wouldn't even open the door for me. I had just woke up from an awful night's sleep when my phone began to vibrate on the nightstand. I saw it was from the car wash, and I picked up immediately. When I heard Yanny on the phone crying I knew something was up.

"Darnell, we been robbed. All the money is gone."

My heart skipped a beat as soon as my phone hit the floor. No, this couldn't have happened to me. No, Yanny had to be lying. Nobody had never robbed me, so this had to be a joke I kept telling myself as I sped through traffic and rushed into my office. All my money was gone from my three safes, and all the money from the register was wiped out also.

Over $100,000 had been taken. There was no point in calling the police because I didn't want them to be counting my pockets and wondering how I was hiding 100,000 dollars and where did it come from. I wasn't risking fucking around with the cops.

"I'm sorry, Darnell. When I left last night, everything was locked up, but when I came in, the window was broken. I came into your office, and that's when I noticed your safes was open and there was nothing in them."

I listened to her as she told me everything she noticed when she first pulled up at the car wash this morning.

I dismissed Yanny as I tried to look throughout my office to see what else was missing. My whole office had been turned upside down. As I began to try to clean up the mess that had been made, I noticed a shiny object on the floor. I picked it up with my hand and studied the diamond stud for the longest moment before the wheels in my brain began to turn. I knew exactly who had been here and who was responsible for robbing me. Rage filled my body as I grabbed my keys and ran out the front door, leaving Yanny and a few of my other employees standing there wondering what had just happened.

I swerved in out of traffic like I was a mad man. I was ready to murder a bitch. A few moments later, I pulled up at my destination and hopped out. I banged on Lexi's door, but the bitch wouldn't answer. I busted the door in and headed inside, only to find the bitch in her room packing her a bag. This bitch had went crazy if she thought I was going to let her ass rob me and leave town.

I balled my fists up and snatched her little ass up.

"Bitch, where my damn money?" I asked her angrily.

She smirked at me which only made me want to kill her ass right then and there.

"I fucked and sucked your dick for six months straight only for you to dip out on me when you all of a sudden wanted to be faithful to your little bitch. You fucked around and got me pregnant. Big mistake, now you about to pay. You ain't about to dismiss me, nigga," she spat at me.

I wanted to straight up murder this bitch. She had lost her fucking mind. I pushed her as down on the floor, and that's when the bitch pepper sprayed my eyes. I screamed as I fell to the floor where she began to stomp me. I tried fighting back, but the pain was too excruciating. When the kicking stopped, that's when I heard her footsteps running out the house and the car pulling out the driveway. It was the grace of the man above that I was even able to get up off the floor. As I washed the pepper spray out my eyes, I began to wish that I would never have stuck my dick into Lexi. Now my money was gone, and she probably had dipped the fuck out of town.

After I had gotten my eyes situated, I hopped back in my car and tried not to look at what had just happened negatively. Instead, I prayed she took that $100,000 and left me the hell alone.

PRINCESS

I had just stepped into the house when I heard Chris Brown (Everybody Knows" blasting from the surround sound. I already knew what was up, and I hated to even go further in to the house because Janae was going to be crying her eyes out. I stepped into the living room and spotted Janae sitting on the couch sipping on a bottle of Cognac and nodding her head to the music. My heart broke as I walked over to where she was sitting and sat beside her. My heart always broke when Janae was hurting. She was like a sister to me, so if she was hurting, so was I. I held her as the tears fell from her eyes.

"I can't believe he did this shit," Janae cried out to me.

"Janae, you doing the right thing. You need to let that nigga go if he ain't going to treat you right."

"I never thought that Darnell would ever do some shit like this to me. The fact he got this bitch pregnant is what killed me. Nothing will ever be the same, Princess. I can never look at him again knowing that he got a seed with another bitch. This the main reason when he tried to persuade me to quit my job that I never did that stupid shit. Niggas can't be trusted. What would I be doing now if I would have listened to him? I would probably be out the fucking door."

"I understand what you saying, boo, fuck that nigga. Focus on you. You got too much going for yourself to accept that shit from him."

"All the shit I sacrificed for him, and this how he going to repay me. I went broke for this nigga. I gave him my all, and he let me down. The way I feel right now, I might be serving life in prison if I ever see his bitch ass."

I left Janae on the couch, headed into her room, and pulled out her medicine. Her and I rolled up a fat blunt and passed it back and forth as we talked about her love life. After the blunt and Hennessy was gone, a knock came at the door. I looked over at Janae whose eyes were bloodshot red. This bitch was higher than a kite. I laughed as I stood up and went to peek outside from the blinds. When I spotted Darnell's Cadillac posted outside, my heart began to race. I looked back at Janae who was laying down on the couch watching a movie on Lifetime.

"Bitch, guess who outside?" I hissed at her.

She sat up and looked at me.

"Who, bitch?" she slurred.

"Darnell," I whispered.

Janae didn't show no reaction at first. I guess his name had to register into her brain before she reacted. Next thing I know this bitch flew to the door and opened it.

Darnell wasn't able to get one word out is lying mouth before she attacked his ass.

I stood back and watched just to see how the shit was going to play out. I mean if he would have laid her ass out I would have jumped in, but this nigga didn't have time to do shit. Janae was giving him a run for his money. Nothing on his face went untouched. She pushed and kicked this nigga with all her force. Janae was short as hell compared to Darnell but she was fucking his ass up. When she kicked Darnell in his nuts, he hollered out because he wasn't expecting her to any fuck with his lower body parts. When he hit the floor, it was over with. She kicked and stomped on this nigga like he was a bitch. I tried pulling her off him, but Janae pushed my ass off her and continued to wreak havoc on Darnell's bitch ass.

Darnell eventually got his dumb ass up and pushed her ass up against the door, but that didn't stop Janae.

"Bitch, are you crazy? I came over here to talk to you, and you acting crazy as hell."

"Nigga, you ain't seen crazy yet! Don't even think I was about to let you bring your bitch ass over here to tell them lies! Now do me a favor and get the fuck out my face!" Janae yelled. Darnell didn't move and Janae resorted to clocking his ass in the eye. When Darnell left, he had a bloody nose and was rocking scratches all over his face.

"And don't your bitch ass come back!" Janae screamed out after him.

Hennessy and some weed had made Janae act a damn fool. I bet Darnell never tried her ass up ever again. It was sad that Janae had to get straight savage on his ass. I could tell when he first stepped inside that he thought he was going to be able to sweet talk Janae into forgiving him, but he was in utter shock when she did the complete opposite. Even though I hated that Janae was hurting, I still felt good that she wasn't weak enough to get back with that bitch ass nigga.

****

A FEW DAYS LATER

It felt good walking into KFC and telling Shay that I no longer was going to be working there anymore. I was grateful that I no longer had to push a clock every day and put up with all those nasty attitudes on a day-to-day basis. Even though what had happened to Janae had cut me deep, I felt in my heart that Darnell and Cameron were on different levels. I felt in my heart that Cameron would never do no fuck shit like Darnell had done with Janae.

My life had been a living hell working at KFC, and I was glad to be moving on to better things. When I stepped back outside and hopped in the car with Cameron, I felt at peace. I felt in my heart that I was doing the right thing by moving in with Cameron and going back to school. When Cameron sealed the deal with that house, I felt like everything that had happened was a reality. Now here I was walking around Ashley's furniture store trying to decide on what type of furniture I wanted to buy for our big ass living room. Cameron was out on the streets hustling with Icey J and had left me his credit card. He told me to buy whatever I wanted, and I was taking this nigga up on his offer. I mean, why shouldn't I?

Cameron and I were living in a 300,000-dollar home. I wanted my house to be on point. I didn't want to have no hand-me-down furniture living in a house that luxurious. I walked around the store and looked at all the different types of living room sets. I couldn't decide if I wanted leather or if I wanted cloth. I was having a debate in my mind when one of the sales men walked over to where I was standing and introduced himself as Mike. He was tall, muscular, dark skinned, and was rocking a clean and trimmed beard. He was cute and everything, but I didn't want to stare at him for too long because I didn't want him to think I was interested.

We walked around Ashley's and he showed me all the different types of living room sets and dining room sets that they had in stock. I eventually decided to go with the three-piece leather set along with a five-piece dining room set that was all black and had a gray marble top. When I pulled out Cameron's black card and told him I was going to pay for it in full, his mouth dropped open. I was spending nearly four thousand on some furniture, but it was going to be worth it. I felt good after I swiped that plastic and told him that I wanted everything delivered the next day. After I left out of Ashley's, I headed to Walmart where I bought stuff to fix up our two bathrooms and three bedrooms. I spent nearly seven hundred dollars at Walmart, and I still felt like it wasn't enough. After leaving Walmart, I headed to the liquor store and got me a bottle of Hennessy before I headed to my new house and started to decorate.

A few hours later, Cameron stepped through the door looking sexy as hell. He walked over to where I was hanging a picture up on the wall and embraced me in a hug.

"Damn, baby, you got the place looking lovely."

I turned toward him and placed a kiss on his lips.

"The furniture is coming tomorrow. If you want to see what I chose, grab my phone off the counter."

Cameron smacked me on the ass before he grabbed my phone off the kitchen island and flipped through my pictures.

"Damn, girl, you picked out some nice shit."

"Thank you, baby. I'm glad that you like it."

"Baby, I love it."

He stepped into the kitchen and held up the bottle of Hennessy that I had purchased earlier that day.

"I wanted to celebrate baby."

"Are you celebrating by yourself?"

"Yes, Janae at work. Do me a favor and pour me some in a glass."

Cameron did as I asked and brought me the half-filled glass of my favorite drink. I sipped on my liquor as I continued to fix up the place.

I looked over my shoulder and watched him as he rolled his blunt up.

"Baby, you know your birthday coming up in a few days. Have you decided what you want to do?"

Cameron stopped what he was doing and smirked.

"For my birthday all I want to do is spend time with you and fuck you until the early morning."

My pussy tingled just hearing him say some shit like that. I gasped when he walked over to where I was standing and smacked my ass before biting my bottom lip seductively.

"I don't want nothing fancy, I just want you all to myself, baby."

"Okay, I can make that possible, boo."

Cameron smirked before he told me he was about to step out on the porch to smoke his blunt that he had just rolled up.

By the time that Cameron stepped back through the door, I had finished over half of the Hennessy that I had purchased. He quickly took the bottle from my hand and didn't hesitate to slide his tongue into my mouth, pick me up, and carry me into our bedroom. Our clothes fell to the floor and I immediately got down on both knees as I began to please him with my mouth. He moaned my name as I sucked and licked the tip of his head. He slid his dick in and out of my mouth in a steady pace as I played with my pussy. I pulled his dick out of my mouth as I showed his balls some love. I was just about to deep throat his dick when my phone began to ring.

"Don't even think about answering it," Cameron groaned.

I continued to suck him off as he slid his dick further down my throat. Tears formed in my eyes, but I didn't dare gag. I swear I gave the best head when I was intoxicated.

"I'm about to cum," he moaned as he pulled my hair tightly into his hands as he pushed his dick deeper into my mouth.

I closed my eyes as he shot his sperm into my mouth. He pulled away from me as I wiped the residue from the corner of my mouth. He was just about to slide in between my thighs when my phone began to ring again. I pulled the phone off the nightstand, and when I saw Janae's name on my screen, I answered without even thinking twice.

“Janae are you okay?” I slurred into the phone.

“No, I’m not okay. I’m broke down on Moody Road. I ran over something and I have no clue how to change a fucking tire. I was wondering if you could come pick me up, but I can tell your ass drunk.”

I looked over at my clock that was located on my nightstand and noticed it was almost midnight. It was late as hell, but I was way too drunk to get my ass out to pick her ass up.

I looked over at Cameron who was laying on the other side of the bed waiting for me to fuck.

“Baby, Janae broke down on Moody Road.”

“What you mean she broke down?” Cameron asked with irritation.

“She ran over something and her tire blew out. Can you please go pick her up and take her home? I’m way too damn wasted to do anything right about now. Matter fact, I feel like I need to go empty my stomach in a few minutes.”

“Girl, stop that shit. You wasn’t too wasted to fuck though.”

I threw a pillow at him before telling Janae that Cameron was on the way to pick her up. I disconnected the call and looked over at Cameron who was grumbling under his breath.

"I don't see why she won't tell her nigga to come pick her up. She need to get rid of his ass because he ain't doing his job."

"Darnell and her are no longer together. There is no way in hell that Janae would call and ask him to do shit for her."

Cameron shook his head at my comment, slid on his Nike sandals, and put on his all white shorts and T-shirt. Even though he was grumbling about picking up Janae, I knew that he wasn't going to be a heartless ass nigga and leave her out there stranded. He placed a kiss on my lips and told me that he was going to be back soon.

I was so wasted that he wasn't even gone for five minutes before my eyes grew heavy and sleep found me.

His hands moved up and down my body just before his hand began to caress my honey box. I moaned as he pulled off my red thong and threw it to the side. When he slid between my legs and began to lick on my clit he had a bitch singing. I gripped the bed sheets as he slid two fingers into my pussy as he continued to lick on my sensitive clit. I closed my eyes tightly and whimpered as my legs began to shake uncontrollably. When I woke up from my dream, I felt disturbed by it, because the nigga who had just made me cum wasn't even Cameron, but really Darnell. My heart was racing, and I was beginning to feel sick to my stomach. Something was wrong. I didn't feel right and the dream that I had just had really creeped me out. There was no way that I would ever do something to hurt my best friend, but I couldn't get over the fact that the dream felt so damn real. I knew deep in my heart something was about to go down, but I had no clue exactly what it was.

CAMERON

A nigga was pissed the fuck off as I headed toward Moody Road. Damn, just when I thought I was about get some pussy, here go Janae calling talking about some bullshit. Hopefully this shit didn't take too long so I could hurry my ass back home so I could slide up in Princess's wet pussy. How drunk her ass was, I already knew her ass was probably passed out. It was dark as hell on Moody, and a nigga couldn't hardly see shit. I quickly put on my high beams and cruised my ass down past Inn Town Suites but didn't see Janae's ass nowhere. I pulled out my phone and dialed her ass up to see exactly where she was. She picked up on the first ring and told me that she was further down the road by the bar and grill. A few moments later, I pulled up behind her car. Janae was posted up by her car and was dressed in a pair of red shorts, a black top, with a pair of black air forces. Her hair was pulled up into a high ponytail, and she was looking sexy as hell. If I wasn't talking to Princess, I would have easily broke Janae off some dick. I instantly felt guilty because I was lusting after my girl's best friend. That was some foul shit, and I instantly pushed her sexy body out of my head.

"I mean, I would change it for you, but it's way too dark out here to even try that shit."

"Don't bother by it. I will send somebody out here in the morning."

I nodded my head at her and told her to hop in the car. She grabbed her phone and locked up her car before hopping in my whip. She was quiet as I cruised toward her place. To be honest, I didn't want to hear no noise anyway; but I could tell how she was looking that she didn't want to be here.

Last time that I was around her was when she had gotten super drunk and was trying to dip out to find Darnell. I just figured that maybe she had ill feelings toward me from then. I loved me some Princess, so I felt like it was my duty to try to get along with her best friend.

I tried making light conversation with Janae, but she wasn't interested. After a while I stopped trying and said fuck it. I was just about to pull up at her spot when her phone began to ring. Janae looked down at her cell and ignored the call. A few more minutes later her phone started ringing again. I swear whoever was calling really wanted to talk to her.

Janae groaned with frustration when her phone started vibrating. I shook my head as she powered down her phone.

"Um, are you okay?"

"Yeah, I'm good."

"You acting all irritated and shit," I told her.

Janae turned toward me and popped her neck.

"Look, right about now I'm not in the mood. You will be irritated too if you was a bitch that was dating a nigga for over two years and you find out that he done got another bitch pregnant."

"Woah, what the hell?"

"Yeah, so you can't tell me nothing about my attitude."

I cursed myself because Princess ain't told me that Janae had left Darnell because of him cheating.

I was speechless because I didn't know what to damn say after she had just told me some shit like that. Now I understood why she was acting crazy that night when he dipped out and didn't come back. Darnell was a damn fool. Janae was too damn fine. I didn't understand why he was out fucking other hoes in the first place.

I pulled up at Janae's spot that she was now living at alone and put my car in park. I looked over at Janae who was wiping her tears from her eyes.

"I'm sorry, Janae, I didn't know. Princess only told me that you and Darnell had broken up, that's it."

"Yeah, it's cool." She mumbled before she grabbed the door to leave.

I grabbed her by her arm to get her attention.

"Janae, I know that you and I aren't close, but since Princess my girl, I feel like it's my duty to at least get to know you."

Janae looked down at her arm and gently pulled away from me.

"Do you truly want to get to know me?"

Janae's body language was speaking volumes to me.

"Of course I do. Why wouldn't I?"

"Because you in love with my best friend. There is no reason for you to get to know me at all."

As she talked I couldn't stop glaring at her sexy lips. Her scent filled my car which had my dick on hard. I moved around in the seat so she wouldn't notice it. I was grateful that it was pitch dark and she couldn't see exactly what she was doing to me. The fact that I haven't had sex really had my dick ready to fuck and having Janae's sexy ass in my car wasn't helping. I was grateful when she stepped out and headed into her place.

As I drove back home, I couldn't get Janae's words out my head.

Deep down inside I knew that I had no reason to get to know Janae. But I had my own selfish reasons why I wanted to become closer to her. I just prayed that Princess never found out how I truly felt about her best friend.

A FEW DAYS LATER

Today was my birthday and my plan was to sleep until I had to get up and head to the trap house later on. I had made plans to be back home by nine so her and I could spend some time together and have some mind blowing sex. I was knocked the fuck out when Princess shook my ass awake. I groaned and tried to pull the covers back over my head, but she wasn't having that shit.

"Nigga, get your ass up and turn on the news."

"Why? What's going on? Can't it wait until I get up?"

"No, nigga it can't wait. I want to know what you did," Princess said.

When she cut the TV volume up, I sat up in bed to see what she was talking about. My heart pounded when I saw the news reporter talking about a body that they had found earlier last night by a jogger in a wooded area in Houston County. When I saw Brianna's picture pop up on the screen, my heart skipped a beat. I watched as the news reporter stated they had no leads. When the chief of police came across the screen and said they wasn't going to rest until the killer was found, I felt his ass was talking directly to me.

Princess cut the TV off and placed her hand on her hips.

"I hope you ain't got nothing to do with her disappearance."

"Princess, I can't believe you going to accuse me of some shit like that. I ain't do that shit."

Princess rolled her eyes at my comment.

"Nigga don't lie to me. That's the same bitch who sent you to jail. Ain't that the same bitch you was so in love with when we first met?"

"You said the right word... was. She ain't my bitch no more, and just because I had a reason to murk her ass don't mean that I did the shit."

"Nigga, stop fucking lying. I know you. Do you think I don't know what you do every day when you leave this house? Don't sit here and treat me like some bitch who don't know shit. You think I don't know what type of person you are? Just because I'm not about that life don't mean I don't know shit about it. I'm not mad that your ass killed her. I'm mad because you ain't tell my ass. I hope your ass didn't leave no type of evidence behind because nigga I promise your ass I will fuck you up myself. I don't want to lose your ass to the system," she said with tears in her eyes.

I was speechless. I pulled her down on the bed next to me and told her that she had nothing to worry about.

"I'm not going anywhere baby. I'm yours forever."

I wiped her tears just before I placed a kiss on her juicy lips.

Princess pulled away briefly as she pulled off her yellow tank top and white pajamas. I pulled my dick out my boxers as she slid back on top of me. Our tongues danced with one another as I slid my rock-hard dick into her tight pussy. She moaned into my ear as I slid in and out of her pussy with a steady pace. I squeezed her ass as I hit her g-spot. Princess sucked on my neck as I pounded her pussy while her juices wet up my stomach.

I pulled out of her and slid between her thighs. I sucked on each of her nipples as I gave her some deep long strokes. She wrapped her legs around my waist as I murdered her pussy. I moaned as she met each thrust that I gave her. When she cried out my name and began to cream on my dick, I pulled my dick out and licked her clean with my tongue just before I slid my dick back into her. I played with her titties and slammed into her honey box until I spilled my seed deep inside her.

I slid out of her, and Princess smirked before finally telling me happy birthday.

"You was supposed to have been told me happy birthday. You woke me up about Brianna being murked, which isn't my problem."

"Well, I'm sorry about that. I just was upset, that's all. But I will make it up to you though."

"How you going to do that."

Princess giggled.

"I can't tell you and ruin the surprise."

I watched her as she slid her fine ass out of the bed and headed toward the bathroom. A few moments later, I heard the shower cut on and instead of joining her, I fell back to sleep.

****

LATER THAT DAY

Since today was my birthday, I decided to head to the trap house for a little while to make some money until I headed back home to spend the rest of the day with Princess. I was in the car with Icey J when Princess hit me up on my cell. I made sure to pick up on the first ring.

"Hey, baby you good?"

"Yes, baby I'm fine. I just got something to ask you,"

"What is it, baby?"

"I know you told me you didn't want to do nothing on your birthday except to fuck, but I invited Janae over so we could have a get together. Don't worry she won't be staying long, she have to work in the morning. I just needed to know what time you coming home tonight?" Princess asked.

"I will be home by nine, and today just another day for me, so I don't care. Do whatever you have planned, baby. As long as we spend time together, that's all that matters to me."

"Okay, baby. Well, I love you."

"I love you to, boo," I said into the phone before disconnecting the call.

Icey J laughed after I slid the phone back in my pocket.

"So when the wedding going to be?"

"Nigga, what you mean?"

"When you and Princess going to tie the knot? You been kicking it hard with shawty and you telling her you love her and shit, so you can't say it ain't serious."

I laughed.

"I'm going to marry her when you marry your girl."

Icey J stared at me and shook his head.

"You going to be waiting a long ass time. You know I'm scared as hell of the M word."

"I don't know why. Marriage is a good thing if you marry the right girl."

"Well, I'm going to let you do the marrying. I ain't with all that."

"Okay cool. Well, once I get married and you see how good it is, I know you going to want to try it."

"Nigga, if you decide you want to jump off the bridge right now, I ain't following your ass to my death."

I swear I almost wrecked the car laughing at his dumb ass.

I pulled up at the trap house a few moments later and we stepped out. People were screaming our names like we was some damn celebrities. I guess we were celebrities because Icey J and I sold the best drugs in War-Town. Icey J and I stayed posted up at the trap all day long. The police rode by a few times, but none of their asses was brave enough to stop and try to say some shit. Music was blasting outside, and bitches was higher than a kite. They was shaking their asses on anybody who was willing to show them some attention. A thick red bone chick walked her ass over to where I was posted up at and began to shake her ass on me. I pushed her ass off of me, and she quickly got the hint and headed over to another available nigga and did the same trick. I watched as the dread head smacked her ass a few times as she twerked on his dick. I shook my head because I never understood what a nigga liked about these dope headed girls that hung out at my trap house all damn day. You really couldn't take none of these hoes serious. All they was looking for was a nigga who was weak for some pussy and use that shit to get their drugs. I mean, I constantly seen bitches sucking niggas' dick and fucking niggas for their powder, but that wasn't none of my business as long as I got paid. I didn't give a fuck what they had to do to get it.

I looked down at the time and noticed it was getting late. I found Icey J and told him I was about to dip out. He dapped a few niggas up and followed me to the car. Icey J lit a blunt and passed it to me. I took a few hits before passing it back to him. We pulled up at Icey J's girl's house ten minutes later and he hopped out.

"I'ma hit your ass up later," Icey J said before he slammed the door behind him.

Soon as I pulled up at my spot I had this feeling that came over me. Something was about to happen, but I had no clue what it was that was about to occur. When I stepped into the house I heard Migos "Danger" blasting from the stereo. Weed smoke filled the living room, and I knew instantly when I saw Princess and Janae that they was going to be high as a kite. I didn't understand why they both got high and decided to mix that shit with alcohol when they knew they couldn't handle the shit. I shook my head when I noticed two empty bottles of Brandy.

I looked over at Princess, and she looked like she was about to fall over at any moment while Janae was up shaking her ass.

"I see y'all fucked the hell up!" I yelled out over the music.

Princess smirked before she stood up and walked over to where I was posted up at. She was dressed in a pair of blue jean booty shorts, a white top, and a pair of her favorite black Nike socks. She didn't have a lot of makeup on, and she had her weave pulled up in a high ponytail. She placed her hand on my lips as she began to suck on my neck. My dick instantly got hard and I didn't hesitate to place my hand on her ass as I pushed her sexy ass up against the entertainment center.

She stared into my eyes before she told me that she had a surprise for me.

Next thing I know Princess called out for Janae to come over.

Janae was high as hell and wasn't even bothered by us. She sipped on her Brandy as she continued to shake her ass to the music. Princess rolled her eyes before she walked over to where Janae was dancing, took her drink from her hand, and pulled her over to where I was standing.

Janae told me happy birthday before looking away from me. I honestly didn't feel comfortable being too close to Janae because I knew that shit would only get me in trouble. Janae was looking fine as hell, and I hated to be looking at Princess's home girl in a sexual way in Princess's presence. I knew from experience to never surround yourself by shit you know could get you in trouble. Hanging around Janae could really fuck up what Princess and I had going on.

Janae was dressed in a pair of tight blue jean shorts, a black top that had a picture of 2pac on it with a pair of black Air Forces. She had her weave flat ironed straight on her head and she had her lips glossed up with some pink colored lip gloss. I nearly fell over when Princess placed a kiss on my lips and turned right around and placed a kiss on Janae's lips.

I stood there not able to wrap my mind around what I was witnessing. I mean, never have I ever thought that Princess and Janae was ever this damn freaky. I watched in amazement as my girl tongued Janae down. My dick was on rock hard and I was ready to see exactly how far this shit was about to go. When Princess told me to follow her and Janae to the bedroom, I swear I was beyond excited. Never had I ever smashed two girls at once, but just looking at their asses swaying from side to side had a nigga feeling like he was in a dream. There was no way that I ever wanted to hurt Princess and fuck around with Janae behind her back, but this was totally different. Princess had no clue that she was making a dream come true. All I wanted was one night with Janae, and I swore in my mind that the attraction that I had for her was going to go away.

When we stepped into the bedroom Janae and Princess were the first to get naked. I walked over to Princess first and kissed her on the lips before asking her if she was really down to do some shit like this.

Princess looked over at Janae and back toward me.

"I already talked with Janae about it and she was down to do it," Princess reassured me.

I looked over at Janae who was staring back at me. I swear I saw the lust in her eyes. I could tell that she was ready to give up the pussy.

"If y'all cool with it then I'm not about to turn this shit down."

Princess didn't hesitate to get down on her knees, pull my pants and boxers down while I pulled my shirt off. My dick was hard as hell as Princess began to stroke my dick with her hands before she put it in her mouth. I moaned as I pulled on Princess's hair as she gave me some sloppy head. When Janae slid her tongue into my mouth I swear I was ready to bust a nut right then and there. I placed my hand on her ass and squeezed it as our tongues danced together.

I groaned when Princess pulled my dick out her mouth and began to stroke it up and down with her hand as she sucked on my balls. Instead of busting my nut like I wanted to, I pulled my dick out her mouth because I wanted to see what Janae could do with her mouth also. Princess stood up and Janae took her spot. I looked down at Janae as she placed her mouth on my dick and began to suck the life out of me. I moaned and closed my eyes as I enjoyed her dick sucking skills. I opened my eyes as I watched Princess played with her pussy on the bed. I pulled Janae up by her hand and kissed her in the mouth before I hit her on her fat ass. I stroked my dick as I watched Janae slide in between Princess's legs. Just watching Princess's facial expression and witnessing her best friend eating her pussy had a nigga ready to fuck.

I bent down as I slid my tongue in between Janae's pussy lips. I sucked and licked on her pussy as she gave Princess some head. I could hear Princess moaning, and then a few moments later Janae pulled away and started moaning out my name as I slid my tongue toward her ass crack.

"Shit," Janae cried out.

I pulled away and asked them who wanted the dick first?

Janae and Princess looked at one another and then toward me.

Princess smirked before she gave Janae the signal to gone on ahead. When Janae slid her fat ass over toward my dick I was excited as hell. I watched her as she closed her eyes as I slid into her from the front. She wrapped her legs around my waist as I slid back and forth into her tight pussy. I swear it was tight as hell. She had a nigga moaning like a little bitch. I played with her titties as I fucked her. Princess took that time and sat down on Janae's face and Janae went to work on licking and sucking on Princess clit.

Princess cried out Janae's name as she pleased her with her tongue. I pulled out of Janae only to tell her ass to turn over so I could fuck her from the back.

Princess slid off Janae's face and got on her knees as Janae began to lick in her ass crack. I grabbed Janae on her hips as I began to slam into her from the back. I wasn't showing her ass any mercy as I blew her back out and gave her some deep dick strokes. I pulled her hair as I murdered her pussy. When she began to cream on my dick I slid out of her and told Princess's fine ass to come and get her some dick. Princess slid between Janae's thighs as I slid into her from the back. My eyes watched Janae as she closed her eyes and played with her titties. When she opened her eyes a few moments later our eyes met. She licked her lips and I began to fuck Princess harder. I made sure to keep my eyes on her the whole time I was hitting Princess from the back. When Janae leaned her head back and her legs began to shake, I busted my first nut in Princess's pussy.

A nigga was tired as hell, and my dick was weak as fuck from the good head and all the good pussy that I had just received. I left Janae and Princess in the bed and headed toward the bathroom so I could clean myself up. After I had wiped my dick off and taken a long piss, I headed back into the bedroom and noticed that Janae and Princess was knocked the fuck out.

I found my boxers, placed a kiss on Princess lips, and pulled them back on before I slid in bed. Janae moaned as I pulled the covers off her so I could slide beside her. I laid in bed for the longest time. Every time Janae moved, her ass always touched my dick, which had me wanting to wake her ass up so I could fuck her one last time. In my mind, I thought that this was going to stop the thoughts in my head about wanting to fuck Janae, but now that I had gotten a sample of her pussy I didn't want to stop fucking her.

Now I wished I would have told Princess no instead of going along with her. My eyes didn't start getting heavy until two in the morning, and a few moments later sleep found me.

JANAE

I woke up with a painful ass headache and my pussy was throbbing between my legs. I groaned as I rolled over and noticed I was in the bed with Princess and Cameron. I looked down at myself and noticed that I was naked. I groaned as the memories began to play out in my head. When I came over to Princess's house last night, I was thinking that I was coming over to chill, but when Princess told me that she wanted to surprise her man with some kinky sex I had no clue that I was going to be used in her plans. At first when she mentioned her plans, I asked her was she sure she wanted to do this. I would have never agreed if she would have been drunk, but she told me this shit when she was sober. She was talking about how she wanted to do something special for his birthday.

Since Princess and I did everything together, I guess she felt we could fuck the same man and each other if that was what needed to be done. The fact that her and I had never done no shit like this had me feeling it wasn't a good idea. All the shit that she could have gotten or did for Cameron for his birthday, she had made up her mind that she wanted to do a threesome instead, which I found strange. But when she told me she wanted to spice up her sex life, I decided to go along with whatever she wanted.

I felt guilty as hell because deep down inside, I was eager to agree because Cameron had a bitch fiending to sample some of that dope dick that I knew he had.

Cameron just had that look about himself that gave off the impression that he had that dick that would drive a bitch crazy. The whole time that Cameron fucked me I enjoyed that shit, and even thought I was high as a kite, I still remembered everything that he had done to my body and every reaction that I experienced. All I truly needed was one time, but when he rolled his ass over and wrapped his arm around my body, my heart began to race and my pussy began to ache for his dick. I knew then that I had fucked up by sampling his dick. He had awakened a thirst in me that could not be filled.

I hated to move him, but I had to get the fuck out of there because if I didn't, I was going to be late for work. I eased his arm from around my waist and my feet were just about to hit the ground when I heard his sexy ass voice ask me where I was going.

I tried covering my exposed body up with my hands, but it wasn't no use.

He eyed me up as he rubbed the sleep from his eyes and looked back at Princess who was still sleeping like she was a newborn baby.

"I don't know why you trying to hide your body. I've seen every inch of you last night."

My body shivered as his lustful eyes roamed my naked body. My pussy tingled as he slid out of bed and walked over to where I was standing.

"I have to go," I choked out.

"I understand, do you need a ride home?"

"No, I'm good, I can manage to get back home."

I really just wanted to hurry the hell up and get the fuck out of there before I did some shit that I later regretted. I searched around for my clothes and quickly put them on. Cameron stared at me the whole time. When I dipped out the bedroom, he followed behind me until I had made it to the front door. He placed his hands on my wrist and pulled me toward him.

"Why you in such a hurry. You didn't enjoy last night?"

My body ached for a repeat of last night, but I ignored the urge that I was feeling inside. I had to remember that Cameron wasn't my man, but Princess's man. She would literally kill me if I ever did some fucked up shit behind her back. Crushing on her nigga was bad enough. I didn't want to take it no farther than I already had.

I looked into his eyes and saw the hunger and desire in them which let me know that he was feeling the same way that I was feeling.

"I enjoyed myself last night. I truly did. I'm not going to stand here and lie that I didn't, but what happened last night can never happen again. Princess only wanted to spice up y'all sex life and to surprise you for your birthday."

"I understand that. And I had an amazing time, but I'm going to keep it real with you. From the moment I first met your ass I was attracted to you, but never would I ever express that shit because Princess have my heart. Last night I had no clue that Princess had planned to give me this amazing threesome and I enjoyed myself, but now I find myself wanting you to myself."

I almost literally fell out because this nigga was brave enough to even tell me this shit to my face. I looked away and he pulled my face back toward him. When his lips met mine, my panties became wet and all the loyalty that I had for my best friend had evaporated. Princess was a distant thought in my mind as his tongue caressed my own. Damn I wanted him in the worst way.

Why he had to belong to my best friend, I cried in my head.

I was stunned when he pushed me up against the front room door and began to kiss and suck on my neck. I wanted to push him off of me, but I didn't have the courage to do anything but take the love that he was throwing at me. When he tried to unbutton my shorts, I gently pushed his hands away.

"Not here, I can't."

Cameron didn't speak at first; he just placed a few kisses on my lips before he stepped back from me.

Finally I could breathe and think clearly. I made sure to fix my clothes neatly on my body before I tried to hurry out the door.

"I want you, Janae, and I know you want me too."

I turned back around and stared at him for a moment.

"I'm not going to lie and act like I don't want you, but I can't do it. At the end of the day, Princess loves you and she is my best friend. The lust that we had, we filled that last night."

I didn't give him time to say anything else before I headed to my car and dipped out.

As I sat in the driveway for a moment I tried to figure out what I was going to do about the feelings that I found myself having for my best friend's man.

I wiped the tears that had escaped from my eyes and headed home so I could get ready for work. Time I turned on my road, I noticed Darnell's car was parked by my apartment building. I groaned as I pulled up at my normal spot and cut my car off. I wasn't even in the mood to deal with his ass right about now. I had enough shit going on with my emotions that I didn't need him coming and making my emotions go haywire; they already wasn't stable.

Soon as Darnell spotted me, he hopped out his car and knocked on my window. I groaned before I stepped out the car and came face to face with the man who had broken my heart. After that ass whopping that I had given him I thought that I was never going to see him again, but here he was standing in front of me.

"Baby, I know you hate me right about now, but I came to tell you that I love with all my heart. Since you been gone I haven't been able to stop thinking about you. I can barely get up in the mornings. I need you in my life. Please come back to me."

“Darnell, I can never forgive you or get back with you. You betrayed me when you cheated, and you got the bitch pregnant.”

“Janae, please listen to me when I say Lexi is never going to be a problem with us.”

“How she won’t be? She got your child, Darnell!” I yelled at him.

Darnell rubbed his hands through his hair before grabbing my hand in his.

“Baby, Lexi is gone she; dipped out of town. She robbed the carwash took all my money out the safes that I had and left. I don’t know where the fuck she at.”

I crossed my arms and stared into his eyes to see if he was lying to me. Then I realized that I didn’t give two fucks if he was lying anyway. I had taken my heart back from him and there was no going back from that.

I pulled my hand from his and told him exactly how I felt about his ass.

“Darnell, I once loved you with all my heart and soul, but now it’s time to do what is best for my heart, and getting back with you isn’t top of the list. I gave you chance after chance to get your shit together, but you continued to let your dick rule your common sense, now you got to live with the consequences. I’m done and over you. You once had my heart, but I snatched that bitch back after you fucked me."

I tried walking away but he ran behind me, still trying to sweet talk me. I stopped in my tracks and eyed his ass up like he was crazy.

"If you love me like you claim you do, then do me a favor."

"What you want me to do, Janae? I will do whatever I got to do to make things right with you."

"I need for you to leave me the hell alone," I replied bluntly before slamming the door in his face.

He banged on the door a few times before he caught the hint and left. I sighed with relief when I peeked out my window and noticed his Cadillac was gone. Now I had to get my mind right so I could get myself ready to head to work and make this paper. There was no way that I was able to miss today because I needed the hours. No longer was Princess living with me and paying her part of the rent. Darnell was going to moving in with me until I found out about the pregnancy shit. I quickly changed my mind, there was no way I was about to let him come to my place and he had done some foul shit like that. I truly didn't want to have shit to do with his ass, but he was forcing me to have to do some shit that I didn't want to do.

Soon as I pulled up at my job I wanted to hop back in my car and head back home. I truly didn't want to go in today. I had a lot of shit on my mind, and working wasn't on it at the current moment. I hadn't even clocked in ten minutes good before I was ripping and running all over the restaurant taking people's orders and serving their drinks. I was tired as hell, and my feet were aching me. I was the first one out the door when midnight hit. I was so thankful that my shift was finally over. I waved at a few of my coworkers bye before I spotted my car in the distance and hurried toward it. I was grateful that our manager always made sure to keep the lights on in the parking lot for the ones who got off when they closed at twelve at night. I was just about to hop in my car when I heard my name being called. My heart began to race as I seen him run over to where I was standing.

"Cameron, what are you doing here?"

Cameron was looking sexy as hell. His dreads were hanging loose, his diamond stud earrings gleamed as well as his diamond stud nose ring. He was dressed in a pair of gray shorts, a black Gucci Mane shirt, with his black and gray Jordans.

"I wanted to talk to you, that's all. Can I come over to your place so we can talk face to face?"

"Where Princess?"

"She home sleeping."

My brain told me it wasn't a good idea to let Cameron come to my house. The smart thing was to tell his ass to leave me alone and forget all the lusty feelings that I was having for my best friend's man. Instead of listening to my brain, I decided to listen to my heart and they always said listening to your heart would always get your ass fucked up.

"I guess you can meet me at my place," I mumbled.

He smiled at me before nodding his head and running back toward his whip and hopping in. I sighed and shook my head as I got into my car and headed to my spot. I cruised throughout traffic as I tried thinking what Cameron wanted to talk about. As I pulled up at my spot he pulled up beside me. We stepped into my place and his lips instantly found mine. No words was spoken as he slid his tongue into my mouth and began to unzip my black khakis that I had on. I stepped out my khaki pants as he picked me up and carried me to my bedroom. As soon as my back hit the bed he began to undress. I watched him as I slid off my thong and finished pulling off my work uniform. When we were both naked, I slid down to the end of the bed as he caressed his semi-hard dick with his hand. I pushed his hand away and quickly slid his dick into my mouth and started sucking him until his toes curled and he was moaning my name. I licked and sucked on his head until I caressed his balls with my spare hand. I slurped and sucked on his dick until he pulled his dick out my mouth and told me to lay back on the bed.

My body was craving his, so when his hands began to caress my body, I felt as if I was about to lose all my senses. I closed my eyes and opened them immediately when he parted my legs and slid between my thighs. When his tongue began to suck on my clit, I felt I was on an all-time high. I moaned out his name repeatedly as I played with my nipples. When he came up from licking my honey box, he placed kisses on my neck and sucked on each of my nipples before he slid into my pussy. I quickly wrapped my legs around his waist as I rocked with his beat. Instead of holding onto him and scratching him like I wanted to, I gripped the sheets as he moved in and out of me. I cried out his name as I played with my clit while he fucked me to oblivion.

When he pulled out of me I instantly missed him, but I didn't have to wait long before he pulled me on top of him and told me to ride his dick. He didn't have to ask me twice, I was ready to ride his shit until he busted. I placed my hand on his chest as I rocked back and forth on his dick while he held on to my hips. I was rocking slowly and was tightening my pussy walls up as I moved back and forth on his dick, eventually he got tired of me slow grinding and was ready to murder my pussy. He quickly smacked my ass as he embraced me in a tight hug and began to slam into my pussy until I was crying and my legs were shaking. He waited until I had finished creaming before he pulled me off of him and placed my legs over my head and entered into me. I groaned as his big dick intruded into my pussy yet again.

I held on to my ass he began to give me some deep strokes. I swear I knew what bitches was talking about when they said they could feel their nigga's dick in their stomach. He played with my titties as he gave me that dope dick. He moved my legs from behind my head and held them in his hand as he began to fuck me harder.

I cried out his name as he slammed into a few more times before he told me he was about to nut. I closed my eyes as he pulled his dick out and skeeted it on my stomach. I laid there for a little while longer because I couldn't damn move. I swear this nigga had fucked me out of commission. He leaned over and slid his tongue back into my mouth before telling me he was about to go get me a rag so I could clean myself up.

After we were both cleaned up we headed back toward the living room where he pulled me into his lap. My heart was filled with guilt because I had just physically betrayed my best friend. When tears began to fall from my eyes, Cameron quickly wiped them away.

"What we did was wrong but, why shit that feels wrong feels so right?" I asked.

"You ain't the only one who feels guilty. I love Princess with all my heart and soul and I don't want to lose her, but she finds out that you and I just fucked behind her back it's going to be a wrap. She going to leave me and…"

I cut him off and slid out his lap.

"She going to stop talking to me, and the friendship that her and I have had since we was kids will be ruined forever and I don't want that shit to happen."

"So what you want to do about us?" Cameron asked seriously.

I looked over at him and walked back toward him and smiled weakly before placing his lips on mine.

"I think that you and I need to stay far away from each other. I believe if we stay away from one another, the feelings and the lust we have for one another will go away."

Cameron was about to speak, but I hushed him as I placed another tender kiss on his lips. Did I love him? I wasn't sure, but the feelings that I was feeling inside my heart was something that I couldn't deny. My heart broke when he walked out my front door because I knew deep in my heart that this was going to be the last time that him and I was ever going to see one another again.

PRINCESS

A WEEK LATER

I had went out my way to make Cameron's birthday something that he was always going to remember forever. Even though I had to talk Janae into helping me out with Cameron's surprise, she came through for me. There was no way in hell was I about to trust a bitch I hardly knew to have a threesome with me and the man that I loved. I trusted Janae with my life, and I knew she would never do no foul shit like bitches who didn't know me would. I was hurt that Janae and I haven't been able to hang like we used to since we had done that threesome. Every time I called she was at work, but I understood why she was always working because I no longer was there to pay my part of the rent, and Darnell and her were over with.

I instantly began to feel guilty about moving away from her when I knew she didn't have the type of money that I now had to keep herself afloat. I was going to make sure that I made it my duty to talk with Cameron to see if him and I could help her out until her lease was up. I mean, that was what friends was for. I knew if she was dating a nigga with money and they was living good she would help me out as well.

As I laid next to Cameron I couldn't help but thank the man above for bringing such a wonderful man into my life. I kissed him gently on his lips before I slid out of bed and hurried into the bathroom so I could get my day started. When I was finished in the shower, Cameron was up, and I could smell breakfast downstairs that was being cooked. My stomach was growling as I got dressed for that day. I decided to wear a yellow top, a pair of my favorite black jean shorts, with my black and yellow Jordans that Cameron had gotten me the week prior. I pulled my weave into a bun before I applied just a dab of makeup, some matte lipstick, eyeliner, and some mascara. I spun around in the mirror a few times and admired how I was looking. My ass was getting a little fatter and I blamed that on Cameron's good dick skills in the bedroom. I headed downstairs and didn't hesitate to give Cameron some kisses. He pulled me into an embrace as he sucked on my neck. I moaned gently as he whispered good morning in my ear.

"What you cooking this morning?"

"Nothing special. Just some waffles, bacon, sausage, and eggs."

"Damn, it sure smell good. I'm starving."

"Well, I hope you ready to eat because the food is ready."

I made sure to fill my plate up and took a seat at our kitchen table. We laughed and talked while we ate. Once our plates were cleaned, him and I washed the dishes together and I followed him back upstairs. I sat down on the bed as I watched him head toward his closet and start throwing out clothes onto the floor.

"Where you headed to?"

"I'm heading over to the trap house early to handle some business. When I get back, you going to have all my attention."

I pouted because I was hoping that he was down to take me shopping.

"Don't start that pouting baby. You must wanted to do something?"

I walked over to where he was standing and placed my hand on his chest and sweetly batted my eyes.

"Yes, I thought that you and I was going to do something together. I wanted you to take me shopping."

Cameron smirked before he walked over to his dresser and pulled out two stacks.

"Here you go baby. You should have told me you wanted to go out to the mall."

"Even though I can't take you myself, I'm gonna make sure you can shop until you can't shop anymore."

I couldn't help but smile at him.

He was such a wonderful man. My smile quickly fell from my face when I looked down at the stack of cash he had just given me. Damn this shit wasn't going to be the same because I didn't even have my right-hand bitch with me. Cameron must have noticed my facial expression because he quickly asked me what was wrong.

"Nothing really. I just miss my girl Janae. She been so damn busy lately, and we ain't spent any time together since your party. Every time I call, she tells me she busy."

Cameron became quiet before he embraced me in a hug.

"Everything going to be okay baby, don't be sad."

"How about you invite her over on a day that she ain't got to work. I can fire up the grill and we can all chill together."

"Yes, I will love to do that. But do you know how to cook on the grill?"

Cameron chuckled.

"Hell yes, girl. It will be so good it will have you licking your fingers."

Cameron brought a smile to my face for a brief moment before I told him exactly what had been bugging me lately.

"Baby, I hate that Janae doing all that working. I mean, her and Darnell are over with so he ain't staying with her to help her pay them bills I left her with. I left her ass in the middle of a contract and I feel horrible. I'm here laying in silk sheets while my girl over there working twelve-hour shifts to keep a roof over her head."

"What you trying to say Princess?"

"I was wondering if you and I could do something to help her until her lease is up. It wasn't right I dipped like I did and not making sure she was good to take care of herself."

Cameron rubbed his chin like he was thinking.

"Baby, I know Janae like a sister to you, so I'm willing to do whatever I have to do to help her out if that will make you feel better."

All the hurt and pain that I was feeling in my heart instantly evaporated and I felt like my old happy self again because I knew my sister, my rider was going to be looked after. After Cameron had dipped out, I didn't hesitate to pick up the phone and call my girl up to tell her the good news.

I tapped my nails on the dresser as I waited for Janae to answer the phone.

My heart jumped when I heard her voice over the phone.

"Damn bitch, I been calling your ass all week long and haven't heard shit from you but a text here and there."

"I'm sorry boo, I just been working, and the little time I do have to myself I be tired as fuck."

"I understand, Janae, and that's why I'm calling you. Look, I first want to tell you that I'm sorry for dipping out on you like I did. I mean, Darnell bitch ass was supposed to have moved in with you, but I never thought shit was going to turn out like it did. I should have waited around until I knew that you was going to be straight. Now you busting your ass all damn day trying to pay them high ass bills by yourself. But I just want you to know that Cameron and I talked earlier this morning and he said he was willing to pay your bills and help you out until you get out that lease. I mean, you my sister, bitch, and there is no way I'm going to be living good and you ain't."

The phone was silent, so I called out Janae's name to make sure she had heard me.

“Janae are you there?” I asked her over three times before she finally spoke.

“I’m sorry, Princess, I was just thinking. Look I really appreciate you offering to help me, but I’m good. I will figure it out on my own.”

“Oh hell nall, bitch. There is no way that I’m about to let your ass suffer over there. Look you going to accept my help whether you want to or not. Now get your ass dressed right now because Cameron just gave me two stacks, and I wanted to go shopping. But you know I hate shopping if I ain’t got my right-hand bitch with me.”

“I can’t go. I have to work,” Janae tried to explain.

“What I told you, boo? I got you. Call and tell them something came up and you can’t come in. I’m going to be pulling up at your spot in another hour, so be ready.”

I didn’t even give her time to reply before I disconnected the call.

JANAE

It had been over a week since I had seen Princess, and I had my reasons why I didn't want to be all up in her face. I mean damn, I had went behind my sister back and had fucked her man when I knew she was in love with that nigga. I looked at myself in the mirror and hated what I saw. Tears fell from my eyes because I was hurting inside that I had done some foul shit like that. I didn't want to take nothing from Cameron because I knew what him and I had done. I wanted to move on and forget him. But every time I closed my eyes at night I couldn't stop thinking of him and how bad I actually wanted him to be my man.

Cameron had all the qualities that that I wanted in a man. He had that street mentality and he had this charisma about himself that you could get lost in. I was thinking the best way to get over him was to stay away from him. He didn't text me, and I damn sure didn't text him.

I wiped the tears that had fallen from my eyes before I picked up the phone and called my job up to let them know that I wasn't going to be coming in today. After I had gotten off the phone, I hopped in the shower to clean myself up before Princess got her ass here.

I decided to put on a pair of skinny legs blue jeans, a pink Nike shirt, with my pink and gray Nikes shoes. I flat ironed my Remy weave and dabbed a little lip gloss on my lips before I heard Princess blowing her horn outside. I made sure to snap a few pictures and post them on Instagram before I grabbed my keys and locked up my apartment before I got into the car with Princess.

Princess and I got to talking and laughing about old times, and my mind pushed Cameron and our betrayal from my brain for that moment. We pulled up at the mall ten minutes later and was lucky enough to find a parking spot. It was Saturday and normally the mall be deep as hell, but today it wasn't as packed like it normally be. We shopped for over three hours straight until we couldn't hold any bags on our arms. We headed out the mall and put all our bags in the car, only to head back in the mall to buy some more shit.

I was over in shoe department looking for some heels when Princess asked me if I wanted to come over this weekend to chill with her. When she told me that Cameron was going to be grilling on the grill I wanted to turn it down and was trying to make up an excuse why I couldn't attend. There was no way I was going to be able to survive being in the same room as him knowing we had fucked one another.

"I don't think that will be a good idea. To be honest I don't even feel comfortable."

Princess squinted her eyes and looked at me and I looked away.

"Okay, what the fuck is going on with you."

I ignored her ass and started looking at some more shoes.

"Why you all of a sudden don't want to be around me or Cameron. You ain't been over since his…"

Princess grew silent and I looked over at her to see why in the hell she had all of a sudden gotten quiet.

"Janae, I'm so damn sorry. I can't believe I've been so selfish."

She pulled me in the corner of the shoe store and lowered her voice to where I only could hear her.

"I now understand why you don't want to be around him. I didn't think about the threesome that I practically forced you to do with me. You ain't been around neither of us since. I'm sorry, sis, to have forced you to do some shit you wasn't comfortable with. You have every right to not want to see Cameron again if you so choose, but please don't block me out your life. You the only bitch I trusted to do some shit like that."

I listened as she told me how much I meant to her and how she just wanted to make her man happy for his birthday. She knew how a typical nigga always dreamed of fucking two bitches at the same time, and she just wanted to try it.

I told her that I was good and eventually caved in and told her that I would come over that weekend. When I told her that shit, her eyes lit up and she embraced me in a hug. An hour later, we walked out the shoe store with over five bags before we headed back to the car and went to get some lunch. Princess didn't drop me off until ten that night, and I was beyond exhausted.

Princess waited until I made it into my apartment before she sped off down the road. I was just about to head to my room when the front room light cut on and I nearly had a heart attack. Anger consumed me when I noticed Darnell sitting in the lazy boy chair. He stood up and walked over to me.

"What in the hell are you doing here?" I asked with frustration.

"I came here to tell you that I'm not letting you go."

I put my purse down and headed to my bedroom. I wasn't in the mood to deal with him at this current moment.

"I know I have done some fucked up shit to you, but I'm telling that I've changed and I want to work things out."

I looked over at Darnell and laughed in his face.

"Darnell, you ain't changed. You just upset and hurt that your ass got caught up. So do me a favor and leave me the hell alone before I call the police on you."

Next thing I know, this nigga wrapped his hand around my throat as he pushed me up against the wall. I felt as if I couldn't breathe and tried to fight him off me, but he was just too strong. Tears fell from my eyes, but it was nothing that I could do.

"I've made a straight fool of myself begging your ass back about that Lexi bullshit. I wasn't lying when I told you that Lexi skipped town with over $100,000 of my damn money. You will never have to worry about that bitch ever again. I told you that from now on I was going to be faithful and loyal to you, but since you don't want to act like a good little bitch and forgive a nigga, I'm going to make you lose everything you care about. I know you fucked Cameron. I seen it with my own two eyes when he creeped up in here. See I was going to keep my mouth shut and forgive you for that shit, but now I don't give a fuck about you. I'm going to tell your girl that you have fucked her man. I wonder what will happen then."

Darnell laughed in my ear before he finally released his hold on my neck. I fell to the floor gasping for air, but the nigga didn't show me any mercy.

He looked down at me and shook his head.

"I loved you, Janae, I truly did. But now I don't give a fuck about you."

"Wait," I tried to tell him, but he left out my room just as quickly as he had come in.

I sat down on the floor crying my eyes out because I didn't have a clue about what I was going to do to make shit right again. I wanted so badly to call the police and get a restraining on his ass, but I knew that would only make shit worse. Instead, I crawled into bed and cried until I fell into a deep sleep.

Darnell

There was no way I was about to let Janae just up and dip out on me just because I had made a few mistakes. I mean, damn, I know I had fucked around and gotten another bitch pregnant, but I told her ass that she would never have to worry about Lexi. But she still didn't want to take a nigga back. I had lost sleep and was trying to do whatever to get my baby back, and I wasn't about to give up on us. I found myself doing a lot of shit that I had never done with any other bitch. I was calling and texting her phone nonstop as well as driving by her house. and that's how I saw her and Cameron fucking around with another.

I drove by her house every damn day to try to keep up with her because it wasn't like she was picking up the phone when I tried reaching out to her. When I spotted Cameron's car parked beside hers, I instantly became suspicious and parked farther down from her apartment. I noticed the living room light on and was grateful that her living room blinds was sort of torn at the bottom because that really helped me to see what in the hell was going on. I hid in the bushes as I peeked from the bottom of the blinds, and that's when I saw them kissing each other. I lost vision of them when they headed into the bedroom.

I went home mad as hell that she was giving my pussy away, and to the very nigga who was supposed to have been her best friend's man. Even though I was pissed, I decided to forgive her because I knew I had done some fucked shit to her to make her want another nigga, but I felt I could use that little bit of information for my advantage. I wanted her to think about what she was doing. Was she going to give me another chance, or was she going to let me tell Princess about her betraying her and sleeping with her nigga. I knew if Janae lost Princess, she was going to lose herself also. They was just that damn close.

****

I had too much shit running through my mind, and I needed to get out so I could stop thinking about Janae and how much I wanted her back in my life. When I pulled up at the strip club I gave myself a pep talk and decided to head into the club find me a bad bitch, take her back to my place, and fuck her brains out. Time I stepped into the strip club, marijuana smoke hit me in the face. I stepped over to the bar and ordered me three beers and headed over to the spot where some of the women was doing table dances. I was ready to spend money on any bad bitch who wanted it. Just when I was about to take a seat, a bad bitch came from off the stage and grabbed my hand and asked if I wanted a dance. She was dark skinned, with a fat ass, thick thighs, with some big titties. Her nipples were covered with stars, and she was wearing a bright red thong with a pair of red spiked stilettos. I followed her to her private table and took a seat as she began to slow grind on me. Kodak Black and Lil' Wayne "Codeine Dreaming" was blasting from the speakers.

I placed a few hundred-dollar bills in her thong as she shook her ass in my face. I was really enjoying my damn self until some dumb ass niggas started shooting in the club. Bitches was screaming and running in all different types of directions as shots rang out all over the club. Whoever these niggas was, they had machine guns. Niggas was shooting back at one another until the police sirens was heard in the distance. Next thing I know, police was busting in and telling everybody to freeze. These niggas around here didn't give a fuck about the police. Not once did these niggas drop their weapons. Instead, they started shooting at the police.

It had to be a way to get up out this bitch I thought to myself.

The stripper who was dancing for me told me that it was an exit in the back, just follow the people that was crawling on the floor. It was dark as fuck, but I told her to hold on to me as I followed a few of the people who I spotted crawling toward the back. This wasn't my battle. These niggas came into this club to murk them a few niggas, and I wasn't one of them. I was grateful when I found the exit sign and got the fuck out of there. I found my car and told shawty she could hop in if she didn't have a ride. She didn't even think about the shit before she hopped her bad ass in the passenger seat. *Damn, the one night that I wanted to go out and have fun the strip club would get shot up*, I thought to myself as I swerved in and out of traffic. I looked over at shawty and asked her where she wanted me to drop her off at.

"Well, I ain't in no hurry to get home. If you ain't got any plans we can always go back to your place and chill."

When she licked her sexy lips, it was a wrap. I was down to take shawty home and break her off some dick if that was what she wanted. I had a lot of frustration to get off my chest, and she seemed like the perfect bitch to do it with.

Ten minutes later I was pulling up at my crib, and shawty stepped out and followed me inside. I didn't even bother by cutting on any lights or trying to make her feel at home. She was only here to do one thing, and that was to give me my next nut. As soon as we made it to the bed, she pulled off her bright red thong and got down on her knees just as I pulled down my boxers. When her mouth covered my dick, I closed my eyes as I imagined her to be my baby Janae. I pushed her head back and forth as she gave me some sloppy head. I pulled my dick out her mouth a few moments later and told her to get on the bed.

Her ass was up in the air and her pretty face was in the pillow. Instead of me smashing this bitch raw I pulled out a condom from my nightstand and slid that bitch on before I slid into her from the back. I didn't show her pussy no mercy as I slammed into repeatedly as she played with her clit with her spare hand.

"Fuck me harder," she cried out to me.

I grabbed shawty by her hips and slammed into her a few more times before she began to scream that she was nutting. I slowed down for a moment, picked her up, pushed her back up against the wall, and began to slip back into her. I pumped into her as she wrapped her long legs around my waist. When it was time for me to nut, I grunted and slammed into her one last time before I filled the condom up. I slid out of her and hurried into the bathroom where I cleaned myself up and grabbed a bath cloth for her to do the same. When we were both cleaned, I checked the time and noticed it was getting late. There was no way I was about to let shawty spend the night, so I signaled for her that I was about to dip out and take her back home. She didn't argue with a nigga. I grabbed a shirt out my closet to give to her to cover her naked body up, and we headed out again.

She gave me directions to her apartment, which wasn't too far from where I was currently living at. It wasn't no more than a fifteen-minute drive from where I lived. When I pulled up at her complex, I reached into my pocket and handed shawty four hundred dollars and told her that I enjoyed. Hell, I wasn't lying. The pussy was good because if it had been trash, I would have not given her shit for that wack ass pussy. She smiled at me before taking her money and dipping out. The whole ride home I couldn't stop thinking about what I had just done. Damn, a nigga had just smashed a bitch I didn't know shit about. I didn't even ask the bitch her name.

When I pulled back up at home I crawled into bed and tried to get some sleep but the whole time I kept thinking about Janae. I had to do something to get her attention. If that meant telling Princess about her backstabbing her, then I was ready to do whatever.

CAMERON

When Princess told me that Janae was finally going to come over and chill with us that weekend, I'm not going to lie, a nigga got real nervous. I didn't know exactly what to expect. I was relieved that Princess was no longer walking around the house looking like she had lost her friend, but it was a big risk being around Janae knowing what had happened between us. Every night when I laid in bed, I couldn't get over the feelings that I was feeling inside. I loved Princess with all my heart and soul, but at the same time I was feeling Janae's fine ass to.

I thought fucking Janae one time was going to cut out all the lust that I was feeling, but it had only made the shit worse. I had been trying hard as hell to not call or text Janae, and so far, I had been doing good by keeping my dick in my pants. I had went plenty of nights not really being able to sleep because I couldn't stop thinking about how I had betrayed Princess and the lust that I was feeling for her best friend.

I was just about to get dressed for the day when Princess busted in the room talking about they had found the person who murdered Brianna. At first I didn't respond, which made Princess get up in my face so she could make sure I heard her.

"Nigga, you heard me right. They just said on the news that Brianna's killer have been found. Apparently, they think it is one of her coworkers who did it."

I stopped what I was doing and looked over at Princess who was staring daggers at me.

"Baby, what you want me to say? You know I don't have nothing for that bitch. She set me up."

"I wasn't expecting you to say nothing. I just want you to know what was going on in the news, that's all."

"But I do want you to take me Kroger's so we can get everything we need for this weekend."

"Of course, baby, you know I got you," I said flirtatiously before smacking her on her pretty little ass.

Princess headed out the room with a smile on her face. I was glad that I was the one who put it there.

We pulled up at Kroger's later on that evening and got everything that you could imagine. We picked up some ribs, steaks, hamburgers, and hotdogs. We got some hot dog buns, hamburger buns, chips, baked beans, and some potato salad. We stayed in Kroger for over an hour as Princess went down each aisle packing the buggy up to the point we had no other room. When it was time to check out, I noticed that the girl who was about to check us out was my old high school sweetheart. Back in the day, she had been my first love. I always thought that she was going to be the girl I was going to marry, but it didn't work out that way. She ended up dumping me for another nigga who she later married while we was still in high school.

She smiled at me and I could tell by her facial expression that she was shocked to see me. I looked down at her ring and was shocked to see a big ass diamond on her left finger which gave me the clue that was indeed still married. When she called out my name and asked how I had been doing Princess looked from her back to me.

"Baby, this is one of my old friends from high school."

Princess smirked and I could tell it was about to be some mess. Instead of trying to catch up with old times, I kept my mouth shut because I didn't want Princess to take any of that shit the wrong way. After we walked out of Kroger's, Princess confronted me in the parking lot.

"Who was that bitch back there?"

I looked at her like *baby don't start this right now. It ain't what you think.*

"She was an old friend back in the day. If you would have let me finish introducing y'all, you would have known that she got married in high school."

Princess rolled her eyes, and I quickly grabbed her fine ass and slid my tongue into her mouth. I caressed her ass as our tongues played with one another we stayed in that position for the longest moment before I came up for some air. After we had put the groceries in the trunk of the car, we headed back home.

Later that night I called Icey J up and invited him over with his girl so we could all chill. Princess tried calling Janae but got no answer. After about three tries, she gave up and told me that she still hoped that Janae was still coming over that weekend.

"Baby, you worried for nothing. Of course she going to come over. Look at the time, it's nine p.m. You know she probably at work."

Princess nodded her head as she headed toward the living room with the drinks and some dip that she had just made. We all laughed, talked, and played cards, until one in the morning. When Princess stood up and told everyone she was going to bed, Icey and his girl stood up also and said they was heading back to the house. I dapped him up while Princess and his girl gave each other a hug. After everyone was gone I followed Princess up to bed.

PRINCESS

The get together...

Cameron had just fired the grill up, and I was in the kitchen getting everything situated in the house. Today was a pretty day, so I decided it would be nice to eat outside and enjoy nature. After I fixed the table cloth on the table outside, I headed back in the house to get the bucket of ice so I could keep our liquor and drinks cold.

"Baby, is Icey J going to stop by with his girl?"

"Nall baby, he just text and told me that he ain't going to make it over here."

I frowned because I had brought all this damn food, and nobody was going to show up but Janae. Cameron must have noticed how I was looking because he quickly placed a kiss on my forehead and told me that we had food to last up a whole damn month and it wasn't going to go to waste.

After Cameron had seasoned the food and had put the food on the grill, I headed inside so I could start cooking on the baked beans. A little while later, my phone began to ring and it was Janae.

"I'm outside."

"Come around back I told her."

We disconnected the call, and I cut the baked beans off and placed a lid on them so I could head aside to find her.

I embraced her in a hug as soon as I saw her. She was looking good as hell. She was rocking a pair of hot pink shorts, a white and hot pink shirt, with a pair of hot pink sandals. She was rocking a pair of black shades, and had her hair pulled up in a bun. Her makeup was on point and she seemed to be glowing.

Janae spoke to Cameron and he waved back at her. I could tell how Janae was looking that she had something on her mind.

"Girl, you need you a drink so you can loosen up."

Janae took a beer from the bucket of ice and popped that bitch open and started sipping on it.

"Baby, if you need me, Janae and I going to be in the kitchen."

"Okay, boo," Cameron replied before turning back toward the grill.

"Janae, what's wrong boo?"

Janae was so spaced out that I had to clap my hands to get her damn attention.

"I'm sorry, boo, Darnell is driving me crazy. I'm trying to decide if I should go to the cops."

"Damn, it's that bad?"

"Yes, it's horrible. He broke into my house a few days ago and choked me out."

I shook my head because that nigga was straight crazy. I didn't know why Janae always got niggas who got obsessed with her ass.

Cameron stepped in the middle of our conversation and looked from one to the other before he asked us who was getting stalked. I pointed my finger to Janae and he stared back at her.

"Who stalking you, Janae?"

Janae didn't speak, so I told him myself.

"Do you want me to handle his ass?"

"Nall, I can handle it myself," Janae said before she stared at me and gave me that look to not say nothing else.

Instead of saying how really felt, I dropped the conversation and started back cooking. An hour later, Cameron told us that it was time to eat. Janae and I both hurried out the kitchen and placed the beans and potato salad out on the table. We said our grace and dug into our food. We was half way done when something told me to look up and that's when I noticed Darnell coming toward us.

"What in the hell?"

"Janae, Darnell is here? Did you invite him?" I asked her.

Janae's eyes grew big and I saw the fear in her eyes. Never had I ever seen Janae scared of anything, so I stopped eating and was ready to get Cameron to get that nigga out my place.

Janae put her fork down and turned around and she was face to face with Darnell.

"What are you doing here, Darnell, how did you even find me?" Janae asked him with attitude.

"I've been watching you, making sure you wasn't creeping with another nigga."

That's when Darnell's eyes left Janae's and landed on Cameron's. I looked over at Cameron who was staring at Darnell like he wanted to murk his ass right then and there. I looked down at Cameron's lap and noticed he had his pistol and was waiting to fire that bitch if shit went left.

"Well if you don't want to leave with me, then I guess it's time to tell Princess the truth." Janae grabbed Darnell by his arm as she tried to grab his ass, but it was too late. I could see the fire in Darnell's eyes and I knew he wasn't about to leave because he had some shit he had to get off his chest.

"Princess did you know your sister, your best friend, been fucking your nigga over there. I seen it with my own eyes."

Everything grew quiet, and I swear I felt as if I was about to pass out. No, there was no way that I was about to believe Darnell's lying ass. He just was trying to do whatever he could to make Janae bow down to him. But when I noticed Janae's tears falling from her eyes and when Cameron stood up and started blasting at Darnell. I knew it had to be true. I sat there in my seat not able to move, tears were falling from my eyes, but I didn't dare move from the position that I was in. Cameron was saying something to me, but I couldn't even hear him. I felt dead inside. The two people whom I loved the most in this whole world had betrayed me, and there was no getting over that shit.

The whole time I had walked myself in this fucking trap when I gave the permission to fuck my man with me for his birthday. Never did I ever see this shit coming. When I snapped the trance that I was in, I slapped fire from Cameron. He grabbed me and held me, but I was so angry I broke free and charged toward Janae. I swear I tried to kill the bitch; I was just that angry. There was no way that I could ever forgive her for this shit. I wanted to beat the bitch to death, but Cameron grabbed me and got me off her ass.

"How could you do this to me? How could y'all betray me like this?" I cried out.

Tears were running down Janae's face and she tried telling me how sorry she was, but I didn't want to hear the shit.

Instead, I stomped toward my house and slammed the door behind both of them. I ran toward my bedroom and closed the door behind me and sat down on the bed as I cried my eyes out. I was so pissed that all I truly wanted to do was take Cameron's pistol and kill them both. I heard knocking at the door, but I ignored it. Instead, I laid cross the bed as I tried to think what was my next move. Should I leave the man whom I had given my heart to, or should I stay and try to work things out with him? What should I do about my friendship with my best friend Janae? Should I leave her trifling ass alone, or should I forgive her since I was some cause of her getting addicted to Cameron's dick? Now I understood what bitches meant when they said never share dick with another bitch. I had learned the hard way that even your sister could betray you for some dick. That shit hurt me to my soul. I wiped the tears from my eyes and fell into a deep sleep.

I don't know how long I slept. All I know was when I woke up it was dark outside. I pulled my phone from under the pillow and noticed I had over twenty phone calls from Cameron and Janae a piece, as well as a bunch of text messages. I slid out of bed, and that's when my head began to kill me. I woke up back to the fact that I had lost not only my best friend, but the man who I loved.

It checked the clock that was sitting on my nightstand and noticed that it was 2:30 in the morning. I slid out of bed so I could head downstairs to get me a glass of water. My mouth was dry, and I was in need of a pain reliever. My body shivered as my feet hit the cold ground. I took one step at a time until I neared the living room. I noticed the TV was playing something on the sports channel and Cameron was stretched out over the couch. I tiptoed into the kitchen trying my best to not wake him, but my reflexes was off and the glass fell to the floor and shattered.

"Fuck," I groaned as I tried to bend down and pick the broken glass off the floor.

"Baby, what you doing in here with no shoes on? Don't touch nothing. Let me clean all that glass off the floor."

I took a step back and watched him as he swept up the glass and threw it in the trash.

"What was you trying to get."

"I was trying to get some water," I said more calmly then I truly felt.

Deep down in my heart I wanted to grab a piece of that glass and slit his throat, but I didn't dare listen to my heart or that little voice in my head because I was going to find myself behind prison bars if I did some shit like that. When he handed me the water out the faucet, I sipped it slowly as he stared at me. After I was done I handed it back to him and was just about to head back upstairs when he pulled me gently by my arms.

"Baby, I'm sorry for hurting you. Please forgive me."

I looked into his eyes and then looked away. Should I forgive him? Should I let this man get away with this betrayal that he had done? Can I stand to stay with him and know he had betrayed me like he has? I pulled away from him and stared into the eyes I once got lost in.

"I honestly don't think I can ever forgive you or Janae. I just want you to know that I will be moving out of this house asap."

I didn't even give him time to respond before I headed back upstairs and left him in the kitchen with his mouth hanging open.

A WEEK LATER

I had done a good job by getting through this week and ignoring Cameron at the same time. I didn't even want to be in the same room with his ass. My heart was suffering a heartbreak that I had never felt before. A heartbreak that I probably would never ever get over. I needed to get away from him. I wanted to get away from Warner Robins and never look back. My pain was too severe, and there was no way I ever wanted to see Janae or Cameron ever again. I had just stepped out the shower and was wiping the tears from my eyes. I was home alone because Cameron was out trapping, and for the first time I was glad that he wasn't nowhere nearby.

After stepping out the shower I picked up my phone, ignored the many text messages that Janae had sent me, and pulled up the internet on my phone. I needed to get away for a few days, so I was eager to book a flight to anywhere that had something available. When I read that Paris, France had a flight that was going to be available the next following day, I quickly booked a ticket and hurried to get dressed so I could start packing for my trip to Paris. After I had ordered a ticket to Paris, I made sure to call a moving crew for the following day to come in and move my belongings to one of their storage facilities until I figured out where I wanted to live when I came back to the United States. After I got off the phone with the moving people, I spent the whole day packing some clothes that I felt I needed on my trip.

When the clock struck eight, I was beyond exhausted and slid into the silk sheets that I had grown accustomed to sleeping on. I was sleeping good as hell until I heard my door open and noticed Cameron's shadow walking toward my bed.

He walked over to me and took a seat on my bed. I raised up in bed as I waited for him to tell me what in the hell he wanted from me.

"I know I hurt you. I wish I could take it all back, but I can't. I'm not ashamed to admit that I was wrong. Janae and I fucked up and we sorry."

I wanted to speak, to reach out to him to tell him that I still loved him, but my heart wouldn't allow me to.

Instead, I let a small tear fall from my eyes and he wiped it away.

"All I ask is you give me one more chance to make things right. I miss you, baby. I love you, baby. My life wouldn't be the same if I didn't have your love."

I licked my lips but kept my head down because I didn't trust myself to look into his eyes. It was time for me to be strong and fight the urge to jump into his arms and take him back like all the other weak bitches would do.

"I can't do this, Cameron."

He didn't speak, he didn't fuss, and he didn't get angry. He just got up and walked out my room. I laid back down and cried myself to sleep.

The next morning, I woke up bright and early and went downstairs to find that Cameron was already gone for the day. I felt relieved that he wasn't going to be here to stop me from leaving. I fixed me a light breakfast, ate, and headed upstairs to take a shower and get dressed for the flight that was going to leave later that evening.

After I had stepped out the shower, I slid on a pair of my white leggings, a pair of pink sandals, with a soft pink top. I dabbed on a little makeup and some lip gloss before pulling my weave into a high ponytail. I took a few pictures and posted to my Instagram before I grabbed my bags and began to take them downstairs so I could put them in the back of my trunk. I came back into what used to be the bedroom that I shared with Cameron and took a seat at his computer desk. I pulled out a sheet of paper, then a pen, and began to write him a letter.

Cameron,

When you get this letter I will be thousands of miles away in a location that I don't want to disclose. I just want you to know that I am safe and I'm not dead somewhere. When you and I first met I fell so deeply in love with you. It was just something about you that drew me to you. The love I had for you was real and I loved you with all my heart and soul, but never would I have thought you would have hurt me like you did.

I understand that you may be sorry but you and I can never come back from this type of betrayal. Never can I ever look at you and not see my best friend staring back at me. Maybe one day I will be able to forgive you but it won't be today and it won't be tomorrow.

I pray that one day you will see just how much I truly loved you, and maybe you already see this but it's too late. There is no going back. I hope life treats you well and I hope one day you find the one you've been searching for. I only want peace. Please don't try looking for me because I don't want to be found.

Love,
Princess

After I had finished his letter, I pulled out another piece of paper and started to write the girl who was like a sister to me. Tears fell from my eyes as I put my pen to the paper.

Janae,

By the time you get this letter I will be far away from Warner Robins. I'm not going to disclose my location because I don't want to be found by you or Cameron. I just want to be left alone and be able to move on with my life peacefully.

I never once thought that our friendship that we shared would end like this. Never did I ever think that I would be writing you a letter telling you goodbye. I know you have been calling and texting me trying to tell me how sorry you are for what you done, but there isn't enough sorry's to make the pain go away. I lay in bed every night and cry myself to sleep because not only did I lose the man whom I loved but I also lost my sister and my best friend. Can I forgive you? I ask myself this question every day and still I have no answer. Maybe one day I will be able to wake up and find it in my heart to get over this heartache that I'm feeling but right about now I have no forgiveness in my heart to give to you. I loved you like a sister and you hurt me to my soul. Maybe one day we will cross paths again but until then I only wish you happiness in life.

Love,

Princess

I wiped the tears from my eyes as I put both of their letters in a white envelope and wrote their name on them. I grabbed my keys and purse and headed downstairs. I laid Cameron's letter on the coffee table knowing this would be the first place that he would look. I headed toward his office, unlocked his safe, and pulled out over five stacks and put it in my purse just before I closed the door of this chapter in my life.

When I hopped into my car, I headed straight to Janae's apartment. I didn't see her car nowhere in sight, so I figured she was probably at work. I parked my car, stepped out, and headed toward her door where I left her envelope under her door.

After I had dropped off her letter I headed straight to the airport so I could get the fuck out of Warner Robins. The whole ride to Atlanta I kept replaying everything that I had went through these past few months, and I began to get emotional. Never would I have ever thought that I would have taken such a big loss this year. When I saw the exit of the airport in the distance, I knew that with everything I had lost, I was only going to get it back very soon.

THE END

CONNECT WITH ME ON SOCIAL MEDIA

•Send me a friend request on Facebook:

https://www.facebook.com/profile.php?id=100011411930304&__nodl

•Like My author page on Facebook:

https://www.facebook.com/ShaniceBTheAuthor/?ref=settings

•Join my readers group, be a part of my book discussions, and win free copies of my books:

https://www.facebook.com/groups/636779069802790/?fref=ts&__nodl

•Follow me on Instagram: shaniceb24

ABOUT THE AUTHOR

Shanice B was born and raised in Georgia. At the age of nine years old, she discovered her love for reading and writing. At the age of ten, she wrote her first short story and read it in front of her classmates who fell in love with her wild imagination. After graduating high school, Shanice decided to pursue her career in Early Childhood Education. After giving birth to her son, Shanice decided it was time to pick up her pen and get back to what she loved the most.

She is the author of thirteen books and is widely known for her bestselling four-part series titled *Who's Between the Sheets: Married to a Cheater*. Shanice is also the author of a three-part series titled *Love Me If You*

Can, two standalones titled *Stacking It Deep: Married to My Paper* and *A Love So Deep: Nobody Else Above You.* In November of 2016, Shanice decided to try her hand at writing a two-part street lit series which was titled *Loving My Mr. Wrong: A Street Love Affair*. Shanice still resides in Georgia where she is a devoted, nurturing, and caring mother of her five-year-old son.

Be sure to LIKE our Major Key Publishing

page on Facebook!